THE
HOTTIE
NEXT
DOOR

ROAD TRIP TO PASSION
by Sahara Kelly, Lani Aames & Vonna Harper

OVERTIME, UNDER HIM
by N. J. Walters, Susie Charles & Jan Springer

GETTING WHAT SHE WANTS
by Diana Hinter, S. L. Carpenter & Chris Tanglen

INSATIABLE
by Sherri L. King, Elizabeth Jewell & S. L. Carpenter

HIS FANTASIES, HER DREAMS
by Sherri L. King, S. L. Carpenter & Trista Ann Michaels

MASTER OF SECRET DESIRES
by S. L. Carpenter, Elizabeth Jewell & Tawny Taylor

BEDTIME, PLAYTIME
by Jaid Black, Sherri L. King & Ruth D. Kerce

HURTS SO GOOD
by Gail Faulkner, Lisa Renee Jones & Sahara Kelly

LOVER FROM ANOTHER WORLD
by Rachel Carrington, Elizabeth Jewell & Shiloh Walker

FEVER-HOT DREAMS
by Sherri L. King, Jaci Burton & Samantha Winston

TAMING HIM
by Kimberly Dean, Summer Devon & Michelle M. Pillow

ALL SHE WANTS
by Jaid Black, Dominique Adair & Shiloh Walker

THE HOTTIE NEXT DOOR

Shiloh Walker

Elisa Adams

Ruth D. Kerce

POCKET BOOKS

New York   London   Toronto   Sydney

Pocket Books
A Division of Simon & Schuster, Inc.
1230 Avenue of the Americas
New York, NY 10020

First Pocket Books trade paperback edition August 2009

POCKET and colophon are registered trademarks of Simon & Schuster, Inc.

For information about special discounts for bulk purchases, please contact Simon & Schuster Special Sales at 1-800-456-6798 or business@simonandschuster.com.

The Simon & Schuster Speakers Bureau can bring authors to your live event. For more information or to book an event, contact the Simon & Schuster Speakers Bureau at 1-866-248-3049 or visit our website at www.simonspeakers .com.

Manufactured in the United States of America

10 9 8 7 6 5 4 3 2 1

Library of Congress Cataloging-in-Publication Data

Walker, Shiloh.
  The hottie next door / Shiloh Walker, Elisa Adams, Ruth D. Kerce. — 1st Pocket Books trade paperback ed.
      p. cm. — (Ellora's Cave anthologies)
  1. Erotic stories, American. I. Adams, Elisa. II. Kerce, Ruth D. III. Title.
  PS3623.A35958H68 2009
  813'.6—dc22   2008050596

ISBN 978-1-4391-0295-4

These stories have previously appeared in Ellora's Cave anthologies published by Pocket Books.

CONTENTS

GOOD GIRLS DON'T

Shiloh Walker

ONE

"Dump him."

Lori looked over the fence at Mike and snorted. "We're getting married in three months, Mike."

"All the more reason to do it now instead of later. Divorce is expensive." He simply stared at her levelly, his wide-set green eyes revealing exactly what he thought of Dirk. Mike Ryan hadn't ever liked Dirk—it was one of the few things the two friends had ever seriously disagreed on.

Lori just arched a brow at him and replied, "I don't plan on getting a divorce."

"He doesn't make you happy. You all but said that."

"He does too," Lori muttered, turning around and leaning against the fence. Crossing her arms over her chest, she stared at the half-finished flower bed. She wasn't pouting. Seriously. Dirk *did* make her happy.

She just.

Hell.

She wanted more from him.

"If he made you happy, you wouldn't look so damn depressed right now."

A thick hank of blonde hair fell into her eyes and she shoved it back with a grimy hand, leaving a streak of garden soil on her forehead. "Couples have fights, Mike. That's perfectly normal."

"That wasn't a fight, Lori. Fights involve you yelling. Him yelling. Not him talking and you just sitting there, listening and looking like you want to cry. Hell, I've seen that happen four times in the past two months. You seem to be getting more depressed all the time and you want me to believe you're happy?"

A warm hand came up, cupping the back of her neck. His thumb rubbed in slow, comforting circles and Lori had to fight the urge to turn around, bury her face against Mike's chest and wail like a baby. "It's complicated," Lori muttered, blinking away the tears stinging her eyes.

No, it wasn't. Not really. But she wasn't about to tell her buddy Mike that the reason she was miserable was because her fiancé treated her like a child who couldn't think on her own.

Over the past year, Dirk had become more and more controlling. Lori had been having little doubts about things for a while, but lately—they weren't little doubts. They were more like Lake Superior–size doubts. Lori hadn't even realized how much he was controlling her until a few days ago.

It was hotter than hell, ninety-five degrees, and the heat index had crept into the triple digits. She was jerking some weeds out of her flower beds, trying to get it done before afternoon came and it got *really* hot. Curls kept springing loose from her ponytail, and her hair was sticking to her neck and face, falling into her eyes. Usually, come summer, she had her hair trimmed into layers that made it a little more manageable and a lot cooler.

She hadn't this year. She had planned to. She'd even had an appointment but had cancelled it because of Dirk. Just like she had let him talk her out of buying a sporty little Mustang and talk her into buying a Corolla. *It gets better gas mileage and it will be a lot easier to maintain.*

Other little things here and there. What sort of clothes she should wear. She'd been offered a job at a special needs school. It had involved a pay cut, but she'd really wanted that job. It wasn't enough of a pay cut that it would have caused her problems. Her folks had passed away a few years ago and left her enough money that she could have afforded the cut.

She could have afforded that new Mustang.

He had always been a bit of a control freak, but over the past year Dirk had become more controlling. He tried to tell her what she should wear, how to style her hair, the proper way to clean the house—she was feeling more and more like his drudge instead of his fiancée.

But even that wasn't all of it. It was like he was trying to take over her life completely. Make her decisions for her. Even the most intimate ones.

More specifically, Dirk didn't think she knew what she wanted in her sex life and basically tried to control that too. *No, we aren't going to the club. No, we aren't going to try this. No, we aren't going to try that.*

They had sex one way, missionary, in the bedroom with the lights out. The sex was wonderful, or it used to be until she started trying to convince Dirk to mess around a little more. To loosen up. Now the sex was just okay. Dirk said it was her imagination.

Any time she asserted herself, just a little, it ended up in a fight. Lori was tired of it. And more, although she didn't want to admit it, she had a sinking suspicion that Mike was right.

Mike might not know the whole story but he saw through her façade of happiness. Mom hadn't. Her friends hadn't. And if Dirk had, he didn't care.

Dirk didn't make her happy and he didn't seem too interested in trying to change that.

Mike watched Lori walk away, her tanned shoulders slumped, her head low.

She'd been getting more depressed by the day, it seemed. Today she'd been crying. He could tell by the faint redness in her eyes and it pissed him off something awful.

Dirk was an ass. Up until the past year, he'd been an ass who made Lori happy, but something seemed to have changed that. Mike hadn't seen any signs that Dirk was messing around and Lori said that wasn't it, but there was something.

Lori wouldn't tell him what, and frankly, Mike didn't care.

The only thing he wanted was to see her actually *look* happy again.

The only thing?

Okay, that wasn't all he wanted. He would love a chance to push her pretty, muscled thighs apart and sink his cock inside her but he wasn't doing that. Sex and friends weren't compatible as far he was concerned.

Especially not the way he liked sex. Lori was the ideal girl next door. Cute, sexy as hell, and funny. She loved the outdoors, loved sports, and as far as Mike was concerned, that was too close to the perfect woman. For him, at least.

She taught kindergarten. She went to church. She was sweet and wholesome, and he wasn't going to risk messing up a friendship by putting the moves on her, even if she hadn't been involved.

Wholesome didn't mix very well with the kind of games he liked. But he still didn't like seeing her look so damn miserable.

"Just dump him," Mike muttered to himself, watching as she disappeared inside.

A week later, Mike's words came back with a vengeance to haunt Lori. She should have listened to him.

If she had listened to him, she wouldn't have had to see *this*.

Wouldn't have to feel like this.

How can this be happening?

That question kept circling through her mind, but oddly enough, in some part of her, Lori really wasn't that surprised.

Lori stood in the doorway, staring into her shadowed bedroom as tears rolled down her face.

That was *her* fiancé. The snarling wolf tattoo on his shoulder that she thought was so sexy, the thick sun-streaked blond hair that he kept cut just a little shorter than she liked.

And their neighbor. The pretty redhead with gray eyes and breast implants. Sara Mattingly.

Dirk and Sara. Together.

Sara was on her knees, her ass up in the air, her wrists cuffed at her back and Dirk was pumping back and forth inside her ass, his hands gripping her hips.

The sound of Sara's gasping scream finally pushed Lori to action. Reaching out, she flicked the light on and watched as Dirk turned his head to look at her over Sara's bound body.

Sara was too far gone and had only noticed that Dirk had stopped moving. "Please . . . please . . . "

With a brittle smile, Lori said, "Go ahead, Dirk. By all means."

Spinning on her heel, she stalked away.

Things felt surreal now. The gut-wrenching pain had faded, replaced by a distant sort of shock. Weird random thoughts kept darting through her mind and only a few of them were related to what was going on in her bedroom.

Her mind jumped to the conference she had left early and she actually started looking for her car keys, thinking maybe she should just go back there. It was a four-hour drive, but it was only nine o'clock. It would be late when she checked in, but she could still get some sleep and go to the last day of the conference . . . yeah. Yeah. That would work.

She finally realized she was still holding her keys, the Tinker Bell charm clutched in her hand so hard that the metal bit into her flesh. She stared at the keys for a minute and then shook her head, trying to clear away the thick fog that had wrapped itself around her brain.

"Need to get going," she muttered, shoving her bangs out of her face.

She didn't quite make it to the front door before Dirk caught up to her. "Lori . . . Lori, wait."

The sound of his voice snapped Lori right out of the nice, comfortable fog. Pain returned, biting and tearing at her heart with razor-sharp claws. With the pain came anger and she spun around to face him as rage bubbled up inside.

Dirk reached for her and light glinted off the titanium bracelet she'd given him for Christmas. She'd spent an arm and a leg on it. He had been wearing it while he fucked their neighbor. For some reason, that made her anger spike irrationally.

Holding up one hand, she whispered harshly, "Don't touch me."

"Lori, please don't go. Let me explain—"

"*Explain?*" she demanded. "There's nothing to explain. I just found my *fiancé* screwing our neighbor."

"Lori—"

"Don't. Okay? Just don't."

Dirk continued to move closer and Lori shifted the keys in her hand, holding them so that her house key protruded between her knuckles as she made a fist. "One more step and you'll be lucky if I don't carve your eyeballs out," she warned, her voice a low, furious snarl.

Lashes flickered over his dark chocolate eyes and Dirk stopped in his tracks. "Lori—"

"Shut up!" Her voice broke on the last word and she snapped her jaw shut, waiting until she knew her voice would be level before saying anything else—until she knew she could keep the tears in check.

"This isn't the first time, is it?"

Dirk didn't say anything. But they'd been together for three years. Lori knew how to read him, even if he hadn't figured out how to read her. The look on his face was answer enough.

It was bad enough that he was screwing around on her, but considering how she had found them—their neighbor was getting the things that Lori had asked for time and again. Dirk had told her each time she wouldn't like it.

Rage and hurt warred inside her, both vying to be let out. Lori didn't know if she wanted to scream or cry. But she wasn't doing either here. Not when she could smell Dirk's sweat and Sara's perfume on his body. And she'd be damned if she let him see her cry.

"I'm leaving," she said icily. "When I get back, I want you both out."

"This is my home, honey." Dirk had that pacifying, soothing tone he used when he thought she was overreacting.

"No. It's mine. It *would* have been ours in a few more days." On Monday, they had an appointment at the bank to add him to the mortgage and Lori was overcome by a sense of relief as she realized just how close she had come to screwing up her life.

She was damn thankful the appointment wasn't until Monday. "Now, though? It's mine, completely mine and it's staying that way. I want you *out*."

She turned around and stalked to the door. His hand closed around her right arm and Lori turned, reacting without even thinking. She swung out and punched Dirk square in the nose. Blood spurted and she relished the sight for one second before turning and opening the door.

Her keys were still clutched in her right hand and she knew a second's disappointment that he hadn't grabbed her other arm instead. She would have liked seeing the nasty cut her key could have gouged down his handsome face.

Her voice shook with fury as she said, "If you're still here when I get back, I'll call the cops."

Then she turned on her heel and stalked out.

* * * * *

I t had been his experience that the voice of an angry woman carried.

This was no exception. Her voice interrupted Mike's contemplation of the late evening sky and just how damn bored he'd become with his life.

Rolling from the hammock, he sauntered around the side of his house to see Lori striding toward her car, and her jerk-off fiancé chasing her. Dirk Morrigan was naked as a jaybird.

Lori, sadly, was not. She looked furious. Even from where he stood, he could see the light of temper in her eyes.

Mike had overheard the sounds of two people going at it from her house and it looked like Lori had just gotten home. She was supposed to be at some teacher thing in Fort Wayne until Sunday. Using his brilliant powers of deduction, he figured that Lori had interrupted something Dirk would rather she never have known about.

"Dumb ass," he muttered. Not only was Dirk a jerk, he was obviously a stupid one.

Leaning against the white picket fence, he called out, "Y'all got a problem?"

Lori turned her head and stared at him. Even across the yard, he felt the power of her stare clear down to his gut. She had the softest, prettiest blue eyes. But right now, she was so damn pissed, they looked like ice. She stood stiff as a board, her hands clenched at her sides.

"No, Mike," she said, her voice brittle and sharp. She cast a narrow look over her shoulder toward her fiancé and added, "No problem as long as *he* is gone when I get back."

Mike glanced toward Dirk and drawled, "Might help if he got clothes on first." Then he noticed the swelling coming up around Dirk's right eye and he grinned. "Lori's got a mean left hook, hasn't she? I'd do what she says, unless you want to see if she can aim as well with her knee as she can with her fists."

Dirk opened his mouth, but Lori cut him off. "If he's smart, he'll get everything he can carry out of my house. Come morning, I'm having a bonfire."

Cocking a brow at her, Mike said, "Kind of a dry summer. Might want to think of another way to get rid of his stuff."

"Do you mind, Ryan? Lori and I need to talk."

Glancing toward Dirk, Mike said, "Actually, you need to get some clothes on. And unless your name is listed on the house payment, I think you'd better do what she says."

"This is a private matter, Officer," Dirk snapped.

"It's *Detective*. And private or not, if she wants you out of her house, you gotta get out." Mike decided this was the most fun he'd had in a long time. He hadn't ever liked Morrigan. Maybe the jerk wouldn't leave willingly. Mike would love to help.

His common sense reminded him it wouldn't look very good if one of the other neighbors reported a domestic disturbance and *he* was involved, but hell. It wasn't like he'd get this chance again, right? Looking at Lori, Mike asked, "You want him out?"

"Oh, I want him out, all right," Lori said. Then she jerked her car door open and climbed inside.

Dirk started after her, and Mike said levelly, "You make one move toward that car, buddy, and you and me are going to have a go. And I really don't want to wrestle you until you've got some clothes." Baring his teeth in a smile, he said, "But that doesn't mean I won't."

For a minute, it didn't look like Dirk was going to listen. But as

Lori pulled away, Dirk swore and turned around, stomping back into the house.

Michael called out, "Be gone in an hour, Dirk."

Dirk turned and flipped him off.

Mike ignored him, focusing instead on Lori's disappearing tail lights.

Well, he sure as hell wasn't bored anymore.

For more than an hour, Lori drove around listlessly. With the window down and Aerosmith blaring, she tried to figure out how long this had been going on. Dirk hadn't been acting any differently, so either he was a hell of a liar—or this had not been going on long.

She ended up parked in the parking lot of Exposé.

The club had opened six months ago, and Lori had told Dirk repeatedly that she wanted to go. *It's not your kind of club, honey.*

Lori knew what kind of club it was.

One of her friends from work was a regular there.

Exposé was a sex club.

She'd heard that damn near any kind of fantasy, no matter how kinky, could be acted out inside those walls. And Lori had a lot of fantasies she wanted to try, but Dirk hadn't ever listened.

Not because he wasn't into it, though. From what she had seen just a little while ago, Dirk was more than into kink. Damn him to hell and back, he knew she'd wanted to try . . . *something*. Anything. Hell, with him, nearly everything. She had tried being subtle, then not so subtle, and he hadn't ever listened.

Lori had an image of Dirk pumping against Sara, his cock shuttling back and forth inside the woman's ass. Her stomach twisted, knotting so hard it actually hurt.

He gave it to Sara.

The hot humiliation of it twisted her stomach into such a hard knot that Lori almost doubled over from the pain.

"Not worth it," she told herself. Sooner or later, she'd believe it.

Tears burned her eyes and she dashed them away impatiently, still staring at the discreet lettering of the sign just above the door. The line seemed to be a mile long and as she watched, several couples were turned away. Exposé was a private club. Nonmembers were admitted, but it was at the bouncer's discretion who he let in and who he turned aside.

There was a second entrance, this one with no line.

A man wearing a simple white shirt with a pair of jeans sauntered up to it, his arm wrapped around the waist of a petite brunette. She was wearing a short, black, strapless sheath and a pair of heeled sandals that laced up over her knees. They nodded at the guy watching the second door and walked right in.

The members' entrance.

They'll never let you in.

Even as Lori reached for the handle, she heard those insidious words inside her head. They circled around, repeating themselves over and over as she climbed from the car and started for the line. She doubted her white T-shirt and jeans were what the women usually wore in there, but still, she didn't turn around.

She headed for the back of the line, her hands tucked inside her back pockets. She tuned out the murmur of voices and the hard, steady beat of music pouring from the club as she tried very hard to think of absolutely nothing.

Taking her place in line, she stood there and waited.

When a hand touched her arm, she jumped and spun around, her heart pounding in her chest.

"Grace."

Her friend was grinning, but as she stared at Lori's face, her grin faded. "Honey, what's wrong?"

Lori blinked and shook her head. "Nothing. Just . . . nothing."

Grace rolled her eyes and said, "Uh-huh. Come on, let's go get a drink and you can tell me all about it."

Resigned, Lori followed Grace into the club. She *really* didn't want to talk about it but Grace wouldn't take *no* for an answer. Besides, she could sit at the bar and get a drink. And just the thought of doing something that Dirk wouldn't like was enough to make her smile. Even if it lasted only a few seconds.

TWO

While they waited for class to start, Lori and Grace took turns working the heavy bag. The impact of her fist against the leather sent a jolt singing up her arm and set her blood to pumping hot and fast. She wore a bandana around her head to hold her hair back.

The day after she'd kicked Dirk out, she'd gone to the salon and had four inches chopped off her hair. The thinner, layered cut was a hell of a lot cooler and curled a lot better. With every snip of the scissors, she had smiled.

"You look a lot happier." Grace drew up one leg and pivoted, striking the heavy bag.

After Grace had finished her roundhouse, Lori took a turn. After she'd kicked the heavy bag, Lori looked at Grace with a smile. "I hadn't realized how much I missed class."

"There's something very therapeutic about butt kicking." The door opened and a short, rotund little guy walked inside. As he did, the senior student got up from the floor and clapped his hands together. "Or getting your butt kicked."

Lori smiled and fell in line with the other brown belts.

After they finished warm up, Lori and Grace fell in across from each other for sparring. "Heard anything from Dirk?" Grace asked as they started to circle each other.

Lori feinted and then kicked toward Grace's padded head. "Nope. Don't want to either."

Grace's hand plowed into her rib cage and Lori fell back with an "Ooomph". She retaliated with a spinning heel kick and a punch. The kick didn't land but the punch did and Grace recoiled, rubbing her belly with one gloved hand.

"Geez. Ask a simple question . . . " But she was grinning around the blue mouth guard.

Lori grinned back. "I sort of expected him to call, but nothing."

They fell silent for a few minutes, trading blows until the whistle sounded. After shaking hands, they retreated to the sidelines and dropped to the mat to watch the other students. "Well, I'm still sort of disappointed you didn't get to burn his clothes."

Lori laughed. "Dirk isn't going to risk his Armanis. I could have told you that. Would have been a fun bonfire, though."

"Keep it down, ladies!"

Lori and Grace looked toward the instructor sheepishly. "Oops," Lori muttered.

Grace just grinned. Waiting until the instructor started working with a couple of junior black belts, she leaned over and said, "So I hear you've been given a trial membership to Exposé. You coming this weekend?"

The whistle sounded. Lori and Grace climbed to their feet and headed back onto the floor. "Not sure yet."

"Don't tell me you're getting chicken."

Lori jabbed at Grace's head. "Bite me."

Grace kicked instead, first a front kick, followed by a side kick. Grace circled away before Lori could counter. "I don't know. I'm just kind of . . . uh . . . "

"Ladies, are you here to chat or train?"

From the corner of her eye, Lori saw Master Leland approaching. "Sorry."

They focused on the class, but afterward, Grace asked, "So you're sort of . . . what?"

They sat in the sauna, stripped down to panties and sport bras. "Restless, maybe? Not sure what I'm looking for there."

"It's who." Lori glanced toward Grace and the brunette shrugged. "You aren't the kind of person who goes to Exposé just because you want to get some kinky sex. You're looking for somebody there. Somebody who can give you what Dirk couldn't. A lot of my friends, I'd tell them they need to accept some of the offers they've received. But you . . . well, you'll know when you need to accept it. Casual sex just isn't your thing."

He was seeing things.

Mike convinced himself that was exactly what was going on. It had to be. Because there was no way in hell Lori was sitting at the bar while one of the local Romeos tried to coax her out on the dance floor at Exposé.

Lori was cute. Lori was sweet. He'd admit, privately, that he'd had a thing for her for years, but because she was cute and sweet, he'd never acted on it. Cute and sweet didn't work very well when it came to the kind of things Mike liked from a woman.

Cute and sweet didn't belong at Exposé.

Ergo, neither did Lori. But she sat at the bar, looking entirely too comfortable.

Lori rebuffed the guy, seemingly more interested in her drink, and while Mike was glad she didn't seem too impressed with the moves being made on her, he'd be even happier if she got up and walked out.

He hadn't seen much of her over the past few weeks. Since she'd tossed Morrigan out on his ass, she hadn't been home too much. The few times he'd looked for her, she'd been gone.

Here? He couldn't help but wonder if this was where she'd been. Mike hadn't been to the club in months so there was no way he'd know unless he asked her.

"I'll do that," he muttered. And then he'd get her the hell out of here.

The crowd moved between them and he lost sight of her head of sunny blonde curls for a second. Weaving through the throng of people, he moved closer, muttering under his breath.

He'd come here hoping to blow some steam and get laid if he could find some woman who didn't bore the hell out of him. He hadn't come so he could drag Lori Whitmore out of here before she bit off more than she could chew.

Damn it, the guys at the door were slipping. They were supposed to do a better job of keeping out those who just weren't cut out for this kind of scene.

Lori sure as hell wasn't and she didn't need to be here.

She sure as hell didn't need to be here alone.

A woman alone in here was considered up for grabs, and Mike doubted she wanted to know exactly how much trouble that could get her into. Lori was too sweet, too cute, too . . . *holy hell*.

Just as Mike broke free of the crowd, somebody tapped Lori

on the shoulder, a girl who looked vaguely familiar to him. Lori spun around on her stool and Mike damn near swallowed his tongue as he took in what she was wearing.

No leather for her.

No, Lori was wearing wine red lace, nearly the same color she had slicked on her lips. The corset was designed to look as through she wore nothing under the lace, but as he moved a little closer, he realized it wasn't pale, soft flesh he was seeing under the overlay of lace but some sort of silky cloth that was nearly the same color as her skin.

The teasing hint of what lay under the corset was enough to make him want to tear the lace and silk away, stripping her bare. He wasn't the only one who had an appreciation for the picture she made. Just before he drew even with her, somebody who looked entirely too familiar slid up to her side and rested a hand on her shoulder.

It was Trask Boyett, one of the more serious club members. Unlike the Romeo from earlier, this one would know how to initiate somebody like Lori. And Mike wasn't about to see it happen.

Hell, no.

"Lori."

She looked away from Trask, her eyes meeting Mike's and widening. A soft flush stained her cheeks but she didn't look away. Her eyes were wide and round with surprise as she stared at him and Mike could only imagine the thoughts racing through her mind.

Looking over her shoulder at Trask, he cocked a brow.

Trask's blond brows rose over his pale grey eyes and he smiled slightly. "You shouldn't let her out alone in here, Mike. You know better."

Lori scowled, looking back at Trask but he had already with-drawn, melting back into the crowd. She returned her gaze to Mike, her brows arching over her soft blue eyes as she demanded, "What in hell was he talking about?"

Mike ignored her, reaching out and closing a hand around her arm. "Come on. You and I are going to have a talk."

She resisted, trying to tug her arm away. "I'm having a drink here."

Mike reached behind her and grabbed the half empty tumbler. He tossed it back, grimacing at the overly sweet taste of rum and Coke. After he'd emptied it, he slammed the glass back on the gleaming mahogany bar. "No, you're not. Come on."

Still, Lori tried to tug away from him so he moved closer and bent low, murmuring into her ear, "You can either walk out of here with me or be carried. Believe me, not too many people will think much of it if I throw you over my shoulder."

Her eyes narrowed and the soft curve of her lower lip poked out in a slight pout, but she fell in step alongside him.

Mike had two choices. He could take her upstairs to the pri-vate rooms. For three hundred bucks, he could rent one until the club closed at four a.m. Or he could take her out to the trellised patio. The patio led out into a maze of hedges that had dozens of little nooks and crannies where they could get some semblance of privacy.

The private rooms were tempting, but Mike didn't want to be alone with her, not as edgy as he felt right now.

So the patio it was.

Exposé was hopping tonight. Most of the good spots in the maze were already taken. They passed three different couples who were in various stages of undress. As they walked past the third, Mike glanced over his shoulder and saw that Lori's eyes were wide and her face was pink.

And she was staring at the three people to her left. The woman was on her hands and knees, her mouth full of one man's cock. Another man was kneeling behind her. Her skirt was pushed up over her butt and the man was riding her slow and easy.

Just before they passed out of sight, the woman jumped as one of her partners spanked her—once, twice, three times—leaving the smooth skin of her ass a soft pink.

Mike finally found what he was looking for, an empty alcove set back a little from the path. It wasn't completely hidden, but it was a little deeper than the other spots.

It was only the illusion of privacy. The maze was set up just for the express purpose of watching, being watched . . . listening to those nearby.

Somewhere behind them a woman screamed in pleasure and Mike got his own little jolt of pleasure as Lori's eyes widened. She hadn't been to the club too often, he decided. And not out in the maze yet, he'd bet.

Good.

"Are you having fun?" he asked casually, letting go of her arm and dropping down onto the padded bench.

"Ahh . . . "

That was all she got out. A series of gasping screams, broken up by the words, *"Yes . . . please . . . spank me . . . yes . . . please . . . Master . . . "* filled the night air and her eyes widened even more.

"You're at a sex club, sweetheart," Mike drawled, stretching his legs out in front of him. "Why do you look so surprised?"

Lori made a face at him. "I know where I am, Mike."

"Do you?" he murmured quietly. Then in a louder voice, he said, "What I'd like to know is what you are doing here."

The blush that had been fading returned full force, staining her cheeks bright pink. But she didn't stammer or try to change the subject. She pushed a hand through her hair and Mike's attention was distracted for a minute as he watched the soft, pale strands float back down around her naked shoulders. He wanted to see her naked, stretched out on his bed, wearing nothing but that soft pink blush and those blonde curls. He could imagine those curls wrapped around his fist and that pretty pink mouth wrapped around his cock.

She spoke and Mike stifled a groan, shifting his legs, trying to ease the pressure against his throbbing cock. It took a minute for her words to make sense and when they finally did, his eyes narrowed. Shoving up off the bench, he closed the distance between them as he growled, "Say that again."

She rolled her blue eyes and made a soft little *harrumph* under her breath. "*I said*, Why do people usually go to sex clubs?" She cocked her head and gave him a challenging look. "I'm sort of surprised to see you here. I didn't know this was your scene."

"You never asked, darling," he drawled. He ran his eyes over her soft, curving form, lingering on the low neckline of her corset. Then he raised his gaze, staring at her pretty, wine red–slicked mouth for a long moment before he drawled, "I don't see the point in advertising where I like to spend my free time."

"And I don't see any reason to talk about where I want to spend mine," Lori said archly. Then she gasped as Mike reached out and hooked his fingers under the lacings on her corset, drawing her closer to him.

He spread his legs as he drew her nearer, bringing her to stand between his knees. Close enough that he could smell her skin and see her breasts rise and fall with each breath.

Mike said, "I wish I'd known you were such a curious little kitten, Lori. I'd be happy to help you out." He reached up, trailing a finger down the smooth curve of her shoulder, lower, along the edge of her lace and silk corset.

She inhaled a deep, harsh breath. It made her breasts rise and fall and Mike let his finger linger in the deep valley between her breasts and murmured, "You don't know what you're getting into, Lori. Go home."

Lori hissed and reached up, smacking his hand away from her. "Don't tell me what to do, Mike. I had enough of somebody trying to control me with Dirk. I'm done with it."

Smiling a little, Mike stood and circled around her, staying close enough that their bodies brushed together with each step. "Is that what this is about? Dirk? I can understand wanting to piss him off, but you shouldn't do something you'll regret just to do it."

Lori whirled on her heel and glared at him. Although she was a good eight inches shorter, she still managed to look down her nose at him. "No, it's not about pissing him off. I don't give a damn about Dirk. I'm here because I've wanted to come since the club opened. I tried to get him to come with me." A small, catlike smile curled her lips and she murmured, "Now I'm glad he didn't."

Mike decided he didn't like that smile. He didn't like the secrets that could be lying just behind that smile. "Lori—"

"Don't presume to tell me what to do," she snapped, spinning on her heel and heading back toward the maze. "You know me well enough to know how much that will piss me off."

Mike reached out and closed both hands around her waist. He stroked downward, cupping his hands over her hips, holding her still as he moved up behind her. He pressed his cock against the soft, rounded curves of her butt, rocking against her. "Maybe I don't know you as well as either of us thought."

He lowered his head to nuzzle her neck. Her head fell to the side and Mike almost groaned against the smooth, pale flesh she exposed. "You come to a place like this, darlin', you're going to get told what to do, sooner or later. Isn't that why you came here?"

"No," she snapped, trying to jerk away from him.

Mike just shifted his grip. Sliding one hand around her hip, he pressed low on her belly. He skimmed his other hand up her side and cupped one breast through the silk and lace. The corset was the real thing, though. Through the layers of fabric and boning, he could barely feel her. But the action wasn't lost on her. He could feel the reaction all through her body. "Yes, it is. You came here because you're curious, but you didn't come because you wanted to dominate somebody, sugar. You want to be on the other end. I can see it in your eyes, but I have to wonder if you really know what you're getting into."

Lori had fallen still. Her breasts rose and fell in a ragged rhythm as her breathing sped up. Slowly, Mike reached between her breasts and freed the heavy cord of wine red silk that held her corset closed. "Do you know, Lori?" he murmured, lowering his mouth to her neck as he loosened her corset.

Raking his teeth down her neck, he whispered, "Anybody could walk up and see me touching you. In a minute, I'm going to have you out of this. Anybody who walks by will see me touching you. You sure you want that?"

He turned her around slightly, moving so that he stood in front of her as he finished unlacing the corset. He slipped her out of it and tossed it toward the bench. "Does it bother you that somebody could see you?" he whispered. Reaching out, he tweaked one nipple, squeezing it between his thumb and fore-finger.

The pebbled flesh was diamond hard and when he touched her, her entire body jerked. A soft, ragged moan escaped her lips. Mike stared into her face, cursing silently at the blind arousal he saw on her face.

So much for scaring her off.

Mike's control was strained to the breaking point, though. He had to do whatever it took to get her out of here, *before* he lost it.

Hearing footsteps on the path, he spun her around so that she faced out. It was Trask who appeared, walking by himself. When he saw Mike and Lori, he came up short, a small grin on his mouth. His eyes dropped lower, studying Lori's naked breasts as Mike reached around her and cupped the full globes in his hands.

"A total stranger is staring at you, Lori," he muttered, lowering his mouth to her ear. He bit down gently on her earlobe before he rasped, "Open your eyes."

Her lashes lifted and he saw her gaze widen as she realized they were being watched. "He likes to watch. You want to give to him a show?"

"I prefer to participate," Trask drawled.

Mike laughed, sliding his hands down Lori's narrow torso so he could cup her hips. "I'm not in the mood to share her," he replied.

"Share?" Lori squeaked.

"Hmmm. Share." Mike freed the button at the waist of her low-slung jeans and said, "Is that one of your fantasies, Lori? One of the reasons you came here? Two men at once? Or maybe you were hoping to add another woman in the mix . . . ?"

"No." She shook her head, still staring at Trask with a mixture of horror and arousal on her face.

The soft skin of her belly rippled under his touch as Mike lowered the zipper of her jeans. He slid the tips of his fingers under the waistband of her silk panties, just barely brushing the soft curls at her mound. "Good to hear, Lori. I'm not much interested in sharing you."

Across the distance that separated them, Trask said, "I don't think you're much interested in having her here period, Mike. Honey, he's just trying to scare you off."

"Fuck off, Trask," Mike said easily. He nudged his hips against the round curves of her butt, letting her feel him. "Does that feel like I'm trying to play games, Lori?"

As he spoke, he dipped his fingers lower, until he could feel the hot, wet folds of her sex. Slowly, he circled the hard nub of her clit, once, twice. Then he pushed inside the snug sheath. She was tight—damn tight—and so hot. Mike could already imagine it, stripping her jeans away, taking her to her hands and knees and working his stiff cock inside her. She'd close around him like a silk fist.

The image was almost enough to make him come inside his jeans, just thinking of it.

But this was Lori. No matter what was driving her right now, Mike knew enough about her type to know she'd regret this sooner or later. And that wasn't a burden Mike was going to bear again.

The women he took knew the score.

Lori still believed in fairy tales. Lori wanted to settle down, get married, live happily ever after. It worked for some people—Mike knew that. But she wasn't very likely to find her happily-ever-after here.

And as much as he wanted to, he wasn't going to satisfy himself with her soft, pale body. Neither was he going to let her get used and tossed aside.

Hardening his voice, Mike pushed his fingers deeper and asked, "Come on, Lori. Is this really what you want?"

The soft, broken whimper he heard from her drove him nuts. Mike tried to find something else to focus on, something other than the warm weight of her body against his, something other than the sweet, seductive scent of her skin, something other than how hot and tight her sex felt around his fingers.

Mike looked over her shoulder and met Trask's eyes. "He's watching you, Lori. I know you. Sex is a personal thing for you, something you don't treat casually. Standing here, in front of somebody you don't know, while I do this—" he emphasized his words with a twist of his wrist, screwing his fingers deeper. "This isn't what you want, Lori."

The hell it wasn't . . . the thought circled through Lori's mind, but she couldn't deny one thing. As much as she enjoyed having Mike's hands on her, she didn't want to be watched.

"Mike . . . "

"You want me to stop?" he murmured. "Or keep going? Because if you hang around here, you're going to get a lot more than this." He circled his thumb around her clit, teasing her closer and closer to orgasm and all the while Trask watched, a hot, hungry little light in his eyes.

She almost closed her eyes and tried to block him.

Almost.

But she was going to have to look at herself in the morning, and Lori wasn't so certain she could do that if she went any further than this.

"Stop." Her voice sounded rusty—totally unlike her own. She swallowed and tried again, this time a little louder. "Stop, Mike."

His hands retreated from inside her clothes and she stood there, breathing raggedly, while he adjusted her jeans and her top. His lips brushed her ear and he murmured, "That's what I figured. Go on home, Lori. This isn't the place for you."

THREE

His words echoed in her head for the next two days.
Lori still couldn't believe what had happened Friday night.

She'd gone to Exposé several times since she'd kicked Dirk out on his sorry ass six weeks ago. While some of the guys hit on her regularly, most of them caught the hint pretty quickly, and the few who didn't she just ignored until they did.

But the first time one of those guys actually caught her attention, Mike showed up.

She couldn't have been more startled to see him there if he had shown up wearing a dog collar and nothing else.

Mike didn't need a dog collar to make him stand out. He did it just by breathing, but then, some people were just like that. They seemed to command attention just by walking into a room. He spoke—people listened. It was just part of who he was.

And *that* was the only reason she kept dwelling on what he'd said.

This isn't what you want . . .

He was wrong. Mike didn't know a damn thing about what she wanted. How could he?

He's only been one of your best friends for years . . . maybe that's how?

Lori scowled. She'd been talking to herself all damn day and it looked like part of her was losing the argument. Mike *did* know her. Did that mean that maybe she was just out looking for excitement and after it was over, she'd regret it?

It had been one of Dirk's arguments when she tried to talk him into taking her to Exposé. She hadn't listened. She'd insisted he was wrong.

But maybe . . .

No. "No." Shaking her head, Lori said it aloud, hoping to convince herself. "Dirk was wrong. Mike was wrong. I know what I want."

And it was something a little more exciting than what she had now.

Maybe she wasn't interested in a gang bang and Mike had proven without a doubt that she wasn't into exhibitionism. But she did want more and Lori knew she could find it at Exposé and that was exactly what she was going to do.

And when you see Mike again? What are you going to say?

"I'm a grown woman and I can do whatever the hell I please."

I'm a grown woman and I can do whatever the hell I please."

Lori chanted it under her breath as she pulled into the parking lot of the club.

"I know what I want. I know what I want. I want . . . "

That. I want that. She saw him the minute she stepped through the door and her breath lodged in her throat.

Mike was leaning against the railing, a longneck held loosely in one hand, his eyes watching the dance floor. Her belly clenched with need and she had a strong urge to walk up to him and wrap herself around him. She didn't though. Even if that was the sort of thing she might normally do, the echo of his words were still too loud in her head.

This isn't what you want.

The way he'd said it—so certain, so sure—like he knew what she wanted, what she needed. Hell, how could he possibly know? Lori sometimes didn't know what she wanted. She just knew that she wanted more than she had. A lot more.

Mike could give it to me.

It came out of nowhere, that certain knowledge. Mike was a good-looking guy—Lori had always known that. He was sexy, confident, and capable. More, he was funny, he could be as sweet as could be, and he was smart. Mike was never boring.

But Mike had never been more than a friend and Lori hadn't ever wanted more.

And damn him, if he hadn't put his hands on her, she might have been able to continue never wanting more. Lori turned away from him, sliding through the crowd and climbing the stairs to the second level. The dance floor there was smaller but suddenly Lori wasn't interested in dancing.

What interested her was downstairs, staring at the dancers with moody eyes. But Lori was going to settle for a drink, or five. Whatever it took to forget how good his hands felt on her. And to forget how certain he was that he knew what she needed.

Five minutes later, she was seated at the far end of the bar. She took another drink of her White Russian and tried to decide if she should just go home.

"You hiding?" The words were spoken directly into her ear, warm breath kissing her flesh.

Lori jumped and spun around, bumping into Trask. He backed up just enough to let her finish turning and then he grinned at her. Lowering his head, he asked, "Mike seen you here?"

She faked a bored expression, lifting one shoulder in a shrug. "How should I know?"

Wide shoulders stretched under a white T-shirt. "Well, he's downstairs and you're up here, hiding in the corner."

"I'm not hiding," she said loftily. "I'm having a drink. I don't feel very social tonight."

"And you came to a club? That's certainly a way to be left alone." He skimmed a finger down one of the skinny straps of her shirt. The layers of gauzy rose were see-through everywhere except for her breasts and sequined, so that it caught the light with every breath she took. "Especially dressed like this. You aren't exactly saying *stay away*, not in that outfit."

Then Trask paused, looking into her face. He cocked his head to the side and murmured, "Well. Maybe from the neck down. Your eyes are saying *leave me alone*. Guess that's how you managed to get left alone here as long as you have."

Lori turned back to her drink and managed to scoot just a little bit away. Trask's hand fell to the side but he didn't walk away. She could still feel his eyes burning into her skin. "I came for the drinks, not the company."

His snort had her skin flushing. "You came because Mike told you not to. You don't much care for being bossed around, do you?"

"Do you?"

He laughed a low, husky sound. "Not one bit. But somehow, I don't think you came here expecting to top somebody, now did you?"

Blood rushed to her cheeks, hot and furious, staining them painfully red. She stared into her drink and mumbled, "Just go away, Trask."

He didn't, though. Instead he called out to the bartender. As a beer was pushed in front of him, he said, "And if I do that, then you're going to have somebody else to deal with. At least I'm not going to try to talk you into going outside with me. Or into a room. Nor am I going to try and talk you into leaving. He might, though."

He being Mike.

Lori turned her head and saw Mike working his way through the crowd. He hadn't seen her yet and she jerked her head around, bending over her drink and trying to make herself as small as possible. Next to her, Trask was laughing. "That's not going to work, sugar."

"Would you just shut up and mind your own business?" Lori snapped.

"But this is so much more fun." From the corner of her eye, she saw Trask wave at somebody. And she didn't need to look to see who it was. She could tell. Her skin burned as Mike's gaze came to rest on her, burning a hole into her shoulder blades.

Sending Trask a sidelong glance, she muttered, "Jerk."

Trask just shrugged. "He would have seen you anyway. Man's got radar when it comes to something he wants." He reached out and skimmed his fingers down her shoulder. "You have fun convincing him you came here for just a drink."

"I don't have to convince him of anything," Lori said, but Trask was already melting into the crowd. By the time Mike reached her side, Trask was lost among the masses.

"What are you doing here?"

Spinning around on her stool, Lori gave Mike a bright, false smile and lifted her drink. "Having a drink. And you?"

"I'm getting ready to haul your ass out of here."

Lori arched her brows and studied him for a minute. Then she shrugged and took a sip, spinning back around to the bar. "No. You're not."

"Didn't we already go over this, sweetheart? This isn't your thing."

Indignant, she spun back around to glare at him. He stood there, staring at her with a condescending look on his face that reminded her all too much of Dirk's reaction when she tried to tell him about something she wanted. "No. *We* didn't go over anything. *You* just decided it wasn't my thing. Shouldn't that be my call?"

He reached up, cupping the back of her neck in a big, warm hand. He lowered his head and spoke directly into her ear. She shivered at the feel of his warm breath dancing over her skin, even as angry indignation filled her when he said, "I'll haul your ass out of here, Lori. Don't think I won't."

She couldn't pull away. It wasn't that he was holding her too tightly, though he did have a good, firm grip on her neck. She just *couldn't* pull away. It felt as though there was something magnetic between them, pulling her closer and closer . . . and closer. Lori felt the warmth of his body against hers and realized she had slid off the stool and was pressed against him.

Damn it. Why in the hell was *he* doing this to her? And why now? Mike was one of her best friends, they'd been friends for a long time. Granted, she couldn't say that she hadn't ever noticed him before on that level. She had. But lately . . .

The scent of him flooded her senses and it was making her light-headed. She licked her lips and fantasized, very briefly, about leaning forward and licking him. Right there, just above the pulse she could see in his neck. Instead, she lifted her gaze and met his. "I'm a big girl, Mike. Aren't you the one who was telling me I needed to find what made me happy? Guess what . . . that's what I'm doing."

"And you've suddenly decided that hanging out at a sex club makes you happy?"

Lori lifted a shoulder. "I don't know. But I really want to find out."

For a minute, he was quiet. He said nothing, just watched her with that intense, probing gaze. Then he reached out and closed his hands around her hips. Her skin started buzzing from that light touch and Lori swallowed her whimper before it could escape. But when he pressed his hips against hers, rubbing his swollen cock against her belly, the whimper slipped past her lips, followed by a harsh, ragged gasp.

"I can help you with that, Lori. You're curious? You want to take a walk on the wild side? I can show you things some of the boys here can't even dream about." He skimmed his lips down her throat then raked the skin lightly with his teeth.

Lori shuddered in his arms, but before she could completely melt against him she pulled away. Wrapping her arms around her waist, she said, "And why in hell do you want to do that?"

A tiny grin curled up the corners of his mouth. Reaching out, he took her palm and placed it against the front of his pants, molding his fingers around hers until she cupped him through the denim then rocked against her. "Well, here's one good reason. Another . . . well, you don't know what kind of trouble you're getting into. I can make sure it's just the sort of trouble you'd like."

He leaned down, taking her mouth with his. He pushed his tongue inside her mouth, tangling it with hers. Heat pressed into heat as Lori rocked against him, and for a second she almost ignored the voice of common sense in her head.

But she was damn tired of guys thinking she needed to be protected against what she wanted. Working her hands between them, she jerked her head to the side and arched away from him. His hands fell away from her hips and as soon as he let her go, she backed away. She boosted herself up onto the stool and turned back to her drink. "Go find somebody else to beat your chest for, Tarzan. I'm not Jane, lost in the big, mean jungle. I can handle myself."

There was nothing but silence, and when she looked back over her shoulder Mike was gone.

But she could feel him watching her the entire night. And every time a guy approached her, she couldn't work up any interest.

H e'd planned to spend most of Sunday lying around watching football and drinking beer. Instead, he spent it brooding and staring out the window as he tried to resist the temptation to go over to Lori's.

Whether it was to apologize or kiss her again, he didn't know. He could still taste her. Silk and spices. That was what kissing her made him think of. She looked too sweet and golden to taste that exotic. She tasted dark. She tasted hot. And she'd been hot, arching against him in a way that had him ready to strip her naked and fuck her blind.

She hadn't left, but she hadn't ever gotten up and danced. And it wasn't for lack of being asked. Lori had sat there for nearly two hours drinking rum and cola, then switching to water.

When she had left, he had followed her outside and watched her climb into her car. He had watched her drive away and felt hollow inside.

He still felt hollow inside.

Didn't change the fact that he didn't want her at Exposé.

If she kept going there she was going to end up getting exactly what she thought she was looking for. Mike didn't really care to see her with one of the guys from Exposé. Mike knew that Lori didn't belong there.

He just had to convince her of that.

When the phone rang close to five p.m., Mike glanced at the number out of habit and almost didn't pick up. It was his partner, Alexander O'Malley, but it was their weekend off. No reason to pick up and he didn't feel very social.

Finally on the eighth ring, he did pick up, grunting an unintelligible greeting into the mouthpiece.

"You sound like you've had one hell of a weekend. Heard you were at Exposé. Have any fun last night?"

"Wasn't there looking for fun. Just wanted a drink," Mike replied curtly. And even if he had been looking for fun, he wouldn't have found it. Lately, Lori was the only woman he wanted and he'd be damned if he went down that road. "What do you want?"

"You sound like you're in a shitty mood."

"I am. What do you want?"

Alex laughed. "Hell, you're being such an ass, I don't know if I want to tell you."

"Fine. Don't." Mike started to hang up the phone and Alex muttered, "Hell, you really are in a shitty mood. I was going to bring a friend over but you'd probably scare her off in this mood."

A friend. Mike knew the translation of that, but for once, he really wasn't interested. What he was interested in was off-limits. "Don't bother. My mood is toxic today."

Alex snorted and said, "Yeah, I noticed." He hung up and Mike hit the disconnect button before tossing the phone over his shoulder. It landed somewhere in the vicinity of the couch.

A few yards away, he saw Lori's back door open. She came out wearing a pair of white shorts and a black halter top. As she carried a garbage bag over to the garage, he was treated to a view of her slender, tanned back. Her skin had always looked so incredibly soft.

Now he knew it was even softer than it looked and the memories of it taunted him. It was one of the reasons he hadn't gotten more than an hour or two of sleep last night.

She moved around the backyard for a few minutes after she'd pitched the garbage bag. She knelt down by the flower beds, plucked a few weeds, moved over to another flower bed and bent over to straighten one of the fairy statues. Mike's eyes were drawn to the taut curve of her butt as she bent over and his cock, already hard and aching, started to throb as he imagined stripping away those neat white shorts and pushing inside her. Her pussy first, teasing her closer and closer to climax. When she was begging and pleading, he'd lube up the tight glove of her ass and take her there.

Over and over, until she was too hoarse and limp to even moan his name.

"Shit," he muttered, turning away from the window and stomping across the floor.

Just go over there. It was such a tempting thought. If last night was any indication, then he had a feeling he could have her naked and under him, or kneeling in front of him . . . bent over the back of her couch . . . the images circled through his mind, one after the other, teasing him. Five minutes. He could get her naked and be inside her in five minutes.

He had wanted just that for years, ever since the cute blonde had moved in next door. He hadn't ever pursued her though. Mike had taken one look into her summery blue eyes and known she wasn't the kind for one night stands and he wasn't interested in anything longer.

Then they'd become friends and it had been a little easier to not think about seeing her naked. And it had taken just one touch to totally ruin that. Mike wasn't sure if he'd ever be able to think of Lori in a purely "just friends" light again.

"You shouldn't have touched her," he muttered, swinging away from the window. He prowled the room, alternating between cursing himself and cursing Lori for showing up at Exposé and messing things up.

Hell. He didn't know if he could keep his hands off her. He wanted her too damn much and if she wasn't one of his best friends, there wouldn't be a problem.

He didn't fuck his friends and he didn't fuck women who didn't know the game.

He stomped over to the window just in time to see her straightening from the flower beds, stretching her arms overhead and arching her back. Her breasts lifted with the movement and her top rode up, baring the smooth, tanned expanse of her belly.

"That's it," he muttered, stalking through the house. Lori was a big girl, right? She had gone to Exposé for a reason and who in the hell was he to tell her she shouldn't? And why in the hell shouldn't he be the one to give her what she wanted? He wasn't some stranger. He was the guy who had wanted her for years. And he'd be careful.

Mike knew how to be careful. Just because he usually didn't like to mess with being careful didn't mean he couldn't. He would be careful with Lori. He wouldn't take more than she was willing to give and he wouldn't push her any further than she was ready to go.

When it was over, it was over. Both of them could walk away without regrets.

Right?

It was faulty reasoning. When his cock wasn't hurting like a bad tooth, he knew he'd find all sorts of reasons why he'd have regrets, but right now, he couldn't think of one.

All he could think was how damn bad he wanted her. The jerk-off boyfriend was out of the picture and Lori had melted under his hands. That was all he needed right now.

Throwing open the front door, he got outside just in time to see her climb into her car and shut the door. By the time she was halfway down the street, Mike had stomped back inside, swearing under his breath.

FOUR

Friday came and went without Lori showing her pretty blonde head at Exposé. Mike knew, because he spent the entire damn evening watching the door. By the time last call rolled around, he had convinced himself that Lori had listened to him the past weekend and decided this wasn't the place for her.

Either that, or he'd scared her off.

Didn't matter, as long as she stayed away.

Despite the fact that he had been this far away from trying to seduce her out of her clothes, Mike knew how bad an idea that would be. People needed to stay in the element they were best suited to. Lori wasn't suited for this.

And this was where Mike was comfortable.

He left the club, telling himself that tomorrow night he'd come back and get laid. That was what he needed to do, but his lack of interest in doing just that was part of the problem. He needed to get his mind off Lori, stop thinking with his cock.

* * * * *

Nearly twenty-four hours later, Mike sat brooding over a half-empty tumbler of whiskey, watching as Trask led Lori out onto the dance floor.

Stop thinking of her! Yeah, sure. That was proving a hell of a lot more difficult than he'd expected.

Trask was one of the few regulars who didn't mind going out on the dance floor. Most of the men stood by on the sidelines, watching the ladies. They weren't there to dance.

Those who didn't mind the dancing used it like it was some part of a mating ritual. Mike figured that was all dancing really was. He'd done the same thing himself and hadn't ever thought twice about it.

At least until he saw Trask dancing with Lori.

Tossing back the rest of his whiskey, Mike pushed his way through the crowd on the dance floor. The song ended before he reached them and another one started up, this one faster, with a hard, driving beat. Trask lowered his head, murmured into Lori's ear but she shook her head, backing away. Her face was flushed. From dancing? Or from whatever Trask had said to her?

She left the dance floor and Trask turned around, coming up short when he saw Mike. A wide grin lit his face and he arched a brow. Gold flashed as the hoop in his brow caught the light. "Hi, Mike."

Mike raised his voice, shouting over the music and leaning in closer to Trask. "I see her leave this dance floor with you, you're going to need a doctor."

Trask shrugged. "Don't worry. She's not interested."

Mike watched as the other man lost himself in the crowd and then he turned, searching for Lori's blonde head. He caught a glimpse of her moving through the outer fringe of the crowd. Keeping that blonde head in sight, Mike started toward her.

She disappeared into the women's restroom and Mike propped his back against the wall opposite the door.

The women's lounge was loud and crowded, just like it had been every other time Lori had been in there.

The bathroom was done in black, white, and red with huge art deco prints on the walls and glossy black vases filled with fresh blood-red roses and sprays of baby's breath.

Lori sat on one of the long black lounges with her legs drawn up, staring at nothing.

Trask had asked her to go for a walk with him. A walk out to the maze.

Lori had declined easily.

She wasn't disappointed in what she'd found at Exposé, but she still hadn't exactly found what she was looking for either. She just wasn't interested in visiting the maze, walking by all those little alcoves with any of the men she'd met here. They just didn't interest her much.

What about Mike . . .

Mike . . . He was a different story altogether, and not one she wanted to think about right now. She pushed thoughts of him out of her head.

Thinking about him lately just made her itchy. She remembered the way he had kissed her when they were in the maze the first time she'd been here, the way he'd touched her the second time he'd seen her here. She remembered that confident, certain way he'd told her she didn't belong here. She remembered how his mouth tasted, how it felt on hers. She remembered the way he touched her, knowing they were being watched, doing it just to prove a point.

All in all, those thoughts worked to make her hotter than hell, *and* madder than hell.

Jerk.

Sexy, mouthwatering jerk, but jerk nonetheless.

For the past week, they had been ignoring each other and as far as Lori was concerned, they could keep ignoring each other. At least until he figured out she didn't need a babysitter.

Maybe it had been the good Samaritan in him that had tried to warn her away. She didn't know. Tried to tell herself she didn't really care.

Except she did. She wanted to feel more of his hands on her body. Wanted to kiss him again, wanted to snuggle up close against him and just lean on him, feeling his warmth and his strength. And she missed her friend. She missed leaning against the fence talking with him and she missed catching a movie with him every now and then. She just plain missed him.

"I need to just go home." Lori was too morose to enjoy the club, and until she could stop thinking about Mike so much she was wasting her time there.

With a sigh, she shoved to her feet and headed for the door, sidestepping the two women in front of her who were locked in a tight clinch. Modesty and privacy weren't big issues at Exposé, Lori had figured that out, but she couldn't see getting that hot and heavy in a public restroom. Even one as nicely kept as this one.

All in all, Lori decided that so far her quest for a little more excitement in her life had been a total waste of time. She hadn't found any excitement, and worse, she hadn't found anybody she really wanted to, ah . . . get excited with. Other than Mike.

Out of the blue, Grace's words came back to haunt her. *You'll know* . . .

When they'd been talking in the sauna a few weeks ago, Grace had told her that she'd know when she met the right kind of guy.

Her gut clenched and Lori blew out a breath. The right guy.

Hell. If she was going by the way her body reacted to Mike, then she'd met the right guy years ago.

He was just determined to protect her from everybody. Including himself.

As she opened the door, she was already digging into the small purse at her side for her keys. It wasn't until she plowed into Mike's chest that she even realized he had been standing there.

Waiting for her, apparently.

"Wow. Do I get another lecture?" she said sardonically as she extracted herself from his hands.

"I just wanted to talk to you."

"Not tonight."

As Lori started to walk away, his hand came up and gripped her arm. "Lori . . . "

She stopped in her tracks and turned to look at him. Carefully enunciating each word, she repeated, "Not tonight. I am tired. I am irritable. I want to be alone."

His eyes narrowed, his mouth tightened, but then he nodded and stepped back, his hand falling away.

Lori turned her back to him and walked out.

When she opened her front door, the last thing she expected to see was Mike and she almost slammed the door in his face just so she wouldn't have to talk to him. She was getting damn tired of his unwanted opinions. However, too many years of being nice kept her from being that rude.

Lori arched a brow as she faced him. "Oh, goodie. Are you here to fuss at me again?"

Mike didn't say a word as he closed the distance between them, moving so close that the tips of his booted feet nudged her bare toes. So close she could feel the warmth of his breath on her face. "I'm coming inside. We're going to have a talk."

Lori snorted. "There's nothing to talk about. I'm a big girl and I can do what I want. And there's nothing you can do about that, Mike. Go away."

She reached out to close the door but he caught it with one hand. With the other, he reached out and jerked her against him, pressing her close. So close, she could feel the long, hard lines of his body against hers. "I said, we're going to have a talk. You want to do it here?" he murmured. He slid a hand down her back and cupped her hip. Holding her still, he rocked his cock against her, sending a series of hot, shivery little thrills racing through her.

"I don't mind an audience. But what about you?" He nuzzled her neck and raked his teeth across the sensitive skin.

"Damn it, Mike." She shoved against his shoulders but he just held her closer. "Fine! Come in."

But if she'd been expecting him to let her go, she'd been hoping for too much. She figured that out real quick as he simply slid his arm around her waist and straightened, lifting her feet off the ground. He stepped inside and kicked the door shut behind him, all without removing his mouth from her neck.

A shaky sigh escaped her as he nuzzled her neck right where it joined her shoulder. "I know what this is about, Lori. You're going to Exposé because you're curious. You're not the first to do that and you won't be the last. Hell, I went because I was curious. I've been doing this quite a while and I can tell you one thing for sure: curious people go there all the time, but they don't usually stay long."

He licked her neck then bit down lightly, just grazing the surface of her skin with his teeth. Lori couldn't stop from melting against him and, honestly, she didn't want to. His touch was . . . sheer heaven.

She had to admit that, even if she was irritated as hell with him. "Then what's the big deal? Why does it matter to you so much? Every time you've seen me there, you look ready to spit nails."

Mike chuckled. Lori could feel the vibration of it against her breasts and her nipples started to throb in reaction. Damn it, even his laugh turned her on. How had he gone from best friend to wet dream material?

"It's a big deal because I don't want to see you getting hurt. I don't want to see you get in over your head." He pulled away, reaching up to cup her cheek in his palm. He rubbed his thumb over her lower lip and Lori felt her heart melt. There was something gentle, almost sweet about the unconscious caress.

But the misty feeling started to evaporate as he continued to speak. "There are guys in the club who'll pull you into their lifestyle, Lori, and some of them have very twisted ideas of pleasure. Even I'll admit that. You get pulled too far in, you may have a hard time finding your way back. I don't want to see that happen to you."

"I'm not going to do anything I don't want to do, Mike."

His gaze lifted until they were staring each other in the eye. Sliding his hand down from her face, he cupped his palm around her neck so he could draw her closer. "That's the whole thing, Lori. You *will* want to do it. Maybe not right away and you might regret it later on, but that doesn't undo what you've already done."

Her irritation was almost as effective as a bucket of cold

water. She arched her back, craning her neck away from him and squirming. "Put me down, damn it." This time he actually did, and she wiggled out from between him and the wall. "I'm capable of thinking for myself, Mike. I'm a big girl and I'm getting damn tired of men who think they know what I want better than I do. I'm tired of men thinking that they know what's best for me. I put up with it from Dirk and that was a big-ass mistake. I am *not* going to put up with it from you."

Mike's eyes narrowed and he stared at her with an icy expression on his face. "Don't you dare compare me to that bastard. I'm just worried . . . "

Lori smiled and said, "You're worried I'll get in over my head, like you just said. Which means you don't really think I can think for myself." She planted her hands against his chest and shoved with all her strength.

He didn't move much and the one step he did take back made her think he was taking it more to humor her than anything else. "I know you can think for yourself, Lori. But what you're looking for there . . . look, it's like a drug. You get into it, you start to crave it. Some people can walk away when they realize it's getting too intense. Others can't. And it can destroy them inside."

"For crying out loud, Mike. All I've done is go dancing there a few times. It's not like I'm running up to any and every guy there begging them to make me their sub or something. I'm not looking for an orgy and I'm not looking for recreational sex on the side. Stop worrying about me so much!"

"If you're not looking for recreational sex, as you put it, what *are* you doing there? What are you looking for?" he demanded.

Lori just glared at him and turned on her heel, stalking away from him. He caught her arm and spun her around. As he crowded her up against the wall, pressing his pelvis against hers, Lori pressed her lips together to keep from moaning aloud. Man, the feel of him—it was something else.

She'd thought sex with Dirk had been good. But Dirk hadn't ever made her feel this hot, not even when he was inside her, bringing her to climax. The look of anger on Mike's face kept fanning the flames of her own anger and Lori had an insane, violent urge to reach up and jerk his head down and kiss him with all the fury she had inside her.

"I don't know. Just *something*." She snarled at him and squirmed against his hold. "Go away, will you?"

"No." He had lowered his head and muttered it against her neck. Then he bit her.

Lori felt the shock of it clear down to her toes. She arched against him, her body taut, then she slowly started to melt against him. She whimpered under her breath and started to rock her hips against his, trying to find a little relief from the pressure building inside.

"You got any idea what you're asking for, little girl?" he murmured. As he spoke, he trailed his fingers down the outer curve of one breast. When she arched into his touch, he cupped her flesh more fully and started to circle his thumb around her nipple.

His other hand rested on her waist, and, as he massaged her breast, he wrapped it tightly around her. "You're out of your league there, Lori," he murmured, lowering his lips to her neck in a slow, gentle caress that was completely at odds with the rage she felt coming from him. "You have no idea of the things a man would want to do with you."

Lori tossed her hair out of her face and dared him. "Why don't you tell me?"

"I will tell you. I'll tell you what I'd do if you were there with me. I'd tie you up. You want to lie there helpless, while I strip you naked and tie you to a table?"

Heat ripped through her at the thought of it. If he thought he'd shock her, he was dead wrong. "Yes."

Against her, Mike stiffened. "That's not you, Lori. That's not how you are. You want to lie there helpless, while somebody uses you like a toy and then just throws you away?" he rasped against her ear.

"You wouldn't use me, Mike." She might not know about the kind of sex he was into, but she did know *him*. "And I'd like to see the man who thinks he could just toss me aside. I've been there once. It won't happen again."

"Stop bringing him into this. He has nothing to do with it." His voice lowered and his hands closed over her waist. "Since you seem so certain, maybe I should give you a taste of exactly *what* you're asking for."

Lori forced a laugh. "You aren't going to scare me away, Mike. Don't even try. You don't have it in you to hurt a woman." Just the thought of him giving her a "taste" was enough to have her thighs going limp with need.

"Really," Mike drawled the word long and slow and then his eyes went dark. She received no other warning, just his mouth closing over hers in a hard, violent kiss.

He jerked her shirt and buttons went flying. Her breasts were naked underneath. Mike's hands closed over her breasts but despite the fury she could taste in his kiss, they weren't cruel. Oh, he was rough. He tugged and twisted her nipples, kneading the plump mounds of her breasts, squeezing them with a force that was just shy of pain.

And Lori loved it.

FIVE

When she moaned into his mouth, Mike was torn between stripping her naked so he could fuck her blind and stripping her naked so he could paddle her ass. Then he'd fuck her blind.

Tearing his mouth away from her, he snarled, "Look, damn it. See how easy it is to leave a mark on you?" There were faint, red marks on her breasts from where he'd handled her so roughly. "You want to know how much worse it can get?"

Incredibly, Lori just smiled at him. She slid her hands up his chest as she rose on her toes and pressed her lips to his. "With you? Absolutely."

As she stared up at him with drowsy eyes, Mike could literally feel the threads of his control snapping one by one. "I can only be pushed so far, Lori. Push too far and there's no turning back."

"Promises, promises."

With a snarl, Mike slid his hands under her shirt and jerked it off. Staring at her naked breasts, he boosted her up and braced her back against the wall. He pushed his thigh between hers, using that to support her weight as he lowered his mouth to her breasts.

Through the thin cotton of her pants, he could feel her. Hot and wet. Scalding him through his jeans. His cock jerked in reaction.

Plumping one breast in his hand, he bent down and nipped her lightly. Her nipple was tight and hard, and her skin tasted sweet. Craving more, he opened his mouth wide and sucked on her nipple, taking as much of her flesh into his mouth as he could.

Lori cried out and arched against him. Mike wrapped his hands around her hips and started to drag her back and forth across his thigh. The feel of her moisture soaking through her clothes and his, the scent of her was an aphrodisiac and Mike lowered her to the ground, intent on getting a taste of her.

He stripped away her pants and panties, using his hands to spread her thighs wide. He held her eyes as he lowered his mouth to her sex. The curls on her mound were trimmed and just a few shades darker than her hair. He nuzzled them for a second and then he licked her. She cried out his name, her hands fisting in his hair. Cupping her ass in his hands, Mike held her and started to spear his tongue in and out. She rocked against him. The taste of her flooded his mouth and he groaned, greedy and ravenous for more.

He pushed away from her and caught her hands as she reached for him. He shoved back up to his feet and stared down at her, struggling to breathe. He was sweating. His heart was pounding a mile a minute. He could still taste her on his lips and he wanted more. He had a bad feeling *more* didn't describe what he wanted. He wanted a hell of a lot more and he was going to want it often.

"Lie down."

Lori blinked, her lashes lowering over her eyes. Then she licked her lips and looked him square in the face. "Where?"

"Right where you are, little girl. If I wanted you some place else, I would have told you."

As she lay down, Mike jerked his shirt off and undid the buckle on his belt. He started to take off his jeans, but decided against that. The minute he was naked, he was going to be on her, hard and fast, and he wasn't ready for this to be over before it started.

Lori lay on the hardwood floor, her hair spread around her head and shoulders. Her nipples were hard, her breasts were full. She had long, well muscled thighs and full hips. Her belly was softly curved. Everything about her seemed to scream sex. He moved so that he was standing at her feet and he nudged them with one of his own. "Spread your thighs so I can look at you."

She stared up at him, her face red. Mike cocked a brow at her. "I'm going to go down on you again in a minute and then I'm going to fuck you until you can't see straight. If you're okay with that, then you should be okay with me looking at that pink pussy."

She sucked in a harsh breath of air, her breasts rising and falling. But she slowly spread her legs. Not wide enough, but it was a start. He knelt between her thighs and pushed them wider. "Like that," he muttered. "So I can see how wet you are." As he spoke, he slid one finger through the glistening wet folds. He looked at her face as he slipped his finger between his lips. "You taste good."

She bucked as he touched her again and Mike laid a hand on her belly. "Be still, Lori." He lay between her thighs, using his shoulders to wedge them farther apart. "Don't come before I tell you to."

"Damn it, I'm about to come *now*."

Mike slid one hand down the outside of her thigh until he could stroke the outer curve of her rump. "If you come before

I say you can, I'm going to spank you." He smacked his hand lightly against her flesh and smiled as she stiffened.

He stared into her eyes while he lowered his mouth to her mound. Circling his tongue around her clit, Mike slid his other hand along the inside of her thigh. When he pushed two fingers inside her, she was already tight and hot, clenching around him. He stroked them in and out, and as he began the fourth stroke, she started making a low, keening sound in her throat.

Mike lifted up and stared at her, cocking a brow. "Don't come."

"Then stop touching me!"

Mike smiled at her and twisted his fingers, screwing them in and out. Lori gasped. He lowered his mouth back to her sex and as he stroked her clit, she erupted. Mike continued to stroke her through the climax and when her eyes opened up, he lifted her up against him. "You came."

"You made me."

"I told you that if you came before I told you to, I'd spank you."

Her eyes narrowed. "You did it on purpose."

Mike bent down and murmured into her ear, "I know." Mike stood and lifted her into his arms. He carried her over to the sofa. One end of the sofa was more of a chaise lounge and he chose that end and sat, stretching his legs out. He stroked a hand up her thigh and murmured, "Turn over."

"I don't think so."

Mike fisted a hand in her hair, drew her head back and took her mouth. He kissed her until she was arching and straining against him. Then he pulled away. "Turn over."

Lori crossed her arms over her chest. Mike smiled. "Last chance."

"And what are you going to do, make me?"

"Yeah." He cupped her in his hand, pushing one finger inside her. Her sheath was hot and swollen, resisting his entry. "You ever been so close to coming, that all it would take was one more touch?" As he spoke, he nuzzled her neck.

Lori shivered against him and arched into his hand, rocking her hips faster against his palm. "Mike . . . "

"That's where I'm going to take you, so close that all you need is one more touch and you'll explode. And I won't give it to you."

That was exactly what he did. Over and over, Mike worked her to the edge of orgasm. Her body was covered with a fine sheen of sweat and she was panting, straining, and arching, begging him to let her come. Mike stopped touching her. He cupped her in his hand and lowered his head, murmuring in her ear. "Turn over."

Her eyes were glassy and she obeyed blindly. Mike stared down at her rump and stroked the taut curves for a minute. She jerked at the first light slap. With the second one, she moaned. The third one, she screamed. Mike nudged her thighs apart and pushed his fingers inside her. The climax ripped through her with violent intensity.

He didn't wait until the tremors passed this time. He surged upward, spilling her onto her back. They took up most of the narrow couch but Mike didn't have time to carry her to the bed, or even move to the floor. His cock was so damn swollen, so damn sore, he was certain he would erupt like a geyser any second.

And he wanted to be inside her when it happened. He dug a rubber out of his back pocket and tore it open with hands gone clumsy. He jerked his jeans open and hissed out a breath as he rolled it down his aching length. He shoved her thighs apart and levered his weight up over her. "Look at me," he ordered.

Their eyes met and held as he pushed inside. She was tight around him and he could feel the slick tissues rippling to accommodate him. He gritted his teeth, and lashed down the urge to come into her hard and fast, over and over, until he exploded. Instead, he let her body adjust to his slowly, sinking into her one inch at a time.

Once he had completely buried his length inside, he sank down against her, pressing his body to hers. He could feel every last silken inch of her naked body pressed against his. Mike slid his hands down, capturing first one wrist then the other and pinning them over her head. "You going to let me tie you down, Lori? Just how far are you willing to let me take you?" he murmured against her ear.

"However far you want, Mike." She arched under him and whimpered, rotating her hips against his. She moaned a hungry little kittenish sound and when he pulled out and slammed back inside of her, the kitten turned into a tigress, arching up and purring.

"You sure about that?" He shifted so that he held both wrists in one hand and reached down with his free hand, catching her thigh and dragging it up so that she was open and exposed. "What if I pull out and tell you to turn around and bend over so I can fuck your ass? You going to let me do that?"

She clenched around him and came with sudden, violent intensity. As the walls of her sheath gripped his cock rhythmically, he lowered his mouth to her and muttered, "I'll take that as a yes."

Lori was still floating back down to Earth as he caressed her buttocks, his fingers sliding between to tease the sensitive opening there. He waited until her eyes cleared a little before he pressed the tip of his finger against her anus. "You're tight. You've never done anal before, have you?"

Her eyes were wide and dark. Mike had a feeling she was both excited and terrified. Just the way he'd prefer it. She licked her lips and shook her head, still staring at him. When he pushed the tip of his finger inside her, she shrieked and shuddered in his hands. "Relax," he murmured. "Don't tense up so much. It will just make it hurt."

"It already hurts." Her voice broke a little on the last word and Mike lowered his lips to hers, kissing her and teasing her back to fever pitch.

"It supposed to hurt some. It's not going to feel like it would if I was fucking your pussy, Lori. Otherwise, what's the point?" He wiggled his finger a little, stretching the sensitive opening and waiting until she relaxed a little more before pushing deeper. "We won't do any more tonight, but if you aren't careful, the next time I take you, it's going to be here. And I won't stop until you beg me to."

Lori's eyes stared into his, panicked and aroused. Mike laughed, rotating his hips against hers, driving his cock deep and fast, then retreating in a slow, teasing glide. "You look ready to beg me now, Lori." He dipped his head and circled his tongue around the edge of her lips, tracing the seam between and slipping inside her mouth for just a ghost of a second before he lifted his head.

Then he moved to her breasts, taking one nipple in his mouth, caressing it with his tongue, teasing it until every touch was a toss-up between excruciating pleasure and excruciating pain. Then he went to the other nipple and did the same thing.

By the time he lifted his head to look down at her, she was

panting, flushed, and he knew just one more touch in the right spot would send her screaming into climax. "You willing to beg, Lori?"

Her eyes narrowed, the fog clearing for just a second. "Hell, no."

"I'll take that as a dare." Their gazes locked and held as he slowly started shafting her. Mike shifted his position so that he wasn't rubbing against her clit and every time she lifted against him, trying to get closer, he moved away. He slowed his thrusts, shortening each one until he was only sinking halfway inside before pulling out.

He kept to that rhythm until she was sweating and straining under him. Each slick curve was dewed with sweat and her eyes were dark and blind, staring up at him with desperation. Against his chest, he could feel the tight little buds of her nipples. Everything inside her was reaching for climax.

"You ready to beg?" he teased. Mike slid his hand down her side, cupping his hand over her hip and lifting her slightly. He squeezed the taut flesh of her ass and murmured, "Beg me and maybe I'll be easy on you when I help myself to your sweet little ass."

"I don't want easy," Lori gasped. Her arms tensed, straining against the grip he had on her wrists.

"You want to come?"

"Hell, yes."

"Then beg me . . . Just say *please, Mike* . . . that's all I need to hear." He pulled out and hoped she'd say it soon. As he sank back inside her, he thought his dick would explode.

She held out another three minutes. Then, as he rolled them to their sides and spanked her butt lightly, she lost control. He let go of her hands and she closed them over his shoulders, her nails tearing into his flesh. "Please, Mike . . . damn it, I can't stand it anymore."

Hell. Me neither. Mike groaned in gratitude and rolled her onto her back again, hooking his arms under hers and gripping her shoulders. With her body braced, he started to plunge into her with hard, deep strokes. On the third stroke, they arched against each other and exploded. Mike swallowed her scream and rode her through the climax until her body went limp, collapsing into the narrow cushions of the couch.

A few minutes passed before either of them made a sound. At Lori's mumbled *Mmmph* Mike raised his head and said, "Huh?"

She smiled at him, her eyes closed. "I thought you said it was supposed to get worse."

"Ahhh. Well, I figured I should take it easy on you at first. I won't hold anything back next time." He shifted down and rested his head between her breasts, cupping his hand over one. He rubbed his thumb back and forth over a pink nipple and watched it pucker and draw tight.

"Promises, promises," she teased. Then she looped her arms around his neck and sighed. "Wake me in a week."

Mike didn't give her a week, but he did give her a couple of hours. They lay on her bed, Lori curled up against his side, Mike stroking his hand through the wealth of thick curls. Her breathing was slow and even, her entire body relaxed, and Mike was burning with the need to roll her onto her back and push inside her.

Literally burning. She shifted against him and he could feel the damp heat between her legs. Her right thigh was draped over his and every time she moved, he could feel her. She was still slick and wet from earlier. Wouldn't take much to pull her atop him and push inside her. She'd take him a little easier this time and he could watch her wake up as she rode him.

Sounded like bliss.

Only problem was that the rubbers were on the damn bedside table to his right and he couldn't reach them without making her move.

"You're awake." She mumbled it against his flesh and reached down, closing her fingers around his erection.

Her hand felt soft and cool. Lori stroked him from base to tip and Mike groaned, arching into her touch. "Shit."

Her hand fell away and she sat up, staring at him with big, sleepy blue eyes. Her curly hair tumbled into her face and she reached up, shoving it back. Mike tugged down the sheet she had pulled over her breasts and stared at her. She looked like a wet dream come true—big blue eyes, sun-streaked blonde hair and ripe, round breasts.

He stared into her eyes as he rubbed the back of his hand across one nipple, watching the flesh pebble under that light touch. She leaned into his touch but instead of taking advantage of it, Mike sat up, keeping his back against the smooth wooden headboard. Now that his arms were free, he could reach the rubbers he'd dumped on her bedside table and he grabbed one, tearing it open and rolling down over his cock without ever looking away from her.

"Straddle me."

Lori touched the tip of her tongue to her lips and squirmed a little. "I uh . . . I think I should take a shower. Brush my teeth."

"Later." He reached out and caught her wrist, pulling her to him. She came slowly, shifting so that she could plant a knee on either side of his hips. His erection throbbed, pressed between their bodies. "Take me inside you now."

She did, slowly, her nails biting into his shoulders. Once she had taken him completely inside her, she moaned and arched. Her breasts lifted and he stared at them, his mouth watering. Her nipples were small, tight and pink. He pushed up onto his elbows and caught one between his lips, sucking it into his mouth.

Lori moaned, her hips jerking and the snug walls of her sex clenched around his cock in a milking caress. He shifted to the other one, using his teeth and his tongue ruthlessly. She pumped her hips and Mike reached up, cupping her ass in his hands and holding her tight against him to keep her from moving.

Mike pulled away and stared up at her with a smile. "Slow down," he murmured. "You're always in such a hurry."

She mewled and leaned down, pressing against him. "You get off on teasing people?"

"Absolutely." He fisted a hand in her hair and drew it aside, baring the long, slender expanse of her neck. Then he leaned forward and raked the sensitive skin with his teeth. In his arms, Lori shivered.

With a smile, Mike did it again, this time biting down lightly in the spot where her neck and shoulder joined. He smoothed his hands down her sides and gripped her hips, pulling her against him as he arched into her. He could feel her heat through the thin latex shield but he hated the barrier. He couldn't feel how wet she was and he wanted to. He wanted to be skin to skin. Badly enough that he almost lifted her away so he could strip the rubber off. Common sense won out but he had to have more than this.

Wrapping his arms around her, Mike shifted, rising to his knees and taking her onto her back. He withdrew until just the head of his cock was inside her and then he plunged deep. Buried inside her, he circled his hips and then withdrew. Lori's nails gouged his flesh and he turned his head, pressing a kiss to the back of one hand. Lori bucked under him and her sheath convulsed around his cock, a series of rippling little caresses, each one gripping him tighter than the last. Mike gritted his teeth and held still, waiting until the urge to come had passed. Or at least eased a little.

"Hold onto me," he whispered. Her arms looped around his neck, holding him tightly.

Moving higher on her body, he started to pump inside her again. Slow, deep strokes—teasing strokes. Lori mewled, circling her hips against his. Mike stopped her by simply pressing down against her, pinning her lower body until she fell still. Then he started all over. He pushed up onto his hands and stared down between them, watching as he entered her. She stretched around him, all pink, wet, and tight.

She jolted under him and he looked up to find her watching as well. She clenched around him and Mike hissed out a breath. She did it a second time, this time with a little smile on her lips. "Don't do that."

Her lids drifted low and a husky laugh escaped her. "Do what? This?" She did it again.

Mike growled and dropped his weight down on her. He started driving into her, hard and fast. A startled scream escaped Lori's lips and Mike swooped down, taking her mouth in a demanding kiss. He nipped at her lower lip. She bit his tongue. Mike fisted one hand in her hair, holding her still.

His other hand cupped a plump, warm breast and he tweaked her nipple, squeezing until he knew she'd be hovering between

pleasure and pain. Lori screamed into his mouth and came. Her
sex tightened around his dick until it almost hurt.

Hard and fast, he rode her. When he felt his climax approaching this time, he let it.

She was still convulsing around him as Mike lay sprawled atop
her, completely spent. After the milking little caresses in her sex
eased, he forced himself to roll off her, but he kept an arm around
her waist so that she ended up on top of him.

"I'm still waiting for it to get worse," Lori mumbled.

Mike laughed weakly. "You're trying to kill me."

D amn it, what are you trying to do, kill me?" Lori tugged
away from his hand and climbed out of bed. Her legs
were so damn weak and wobbly that she could barely
stand up. Her stomach was an aching, empty pit and if she didn't
get caffeine soon, she knew things were going to get ugly.

Mike's hand finally fell away from her wrist, and as she dug
a T-shirt out of her drawer she looked back at him. Her heart
skipped a beat at the sight of him. He sat with his back against
the headboard, tan skin gleaming against the soft baby blue of
her sheets. A wicked smile curved his lips and his eyes had that
heavy-lidded, sleepy look. Damn, he was sexy.

He'd pulled the sheet over his lap but as she stared at him, he
fisted his hand in the sheet and tugged it away. Then he brought
his hand to his cock, wrapped his fingers around the thick, swollen flesh and stroked upward. As his fist swallowed the rounded
head, Lori realized her mouth was watering.

"You're evil."

She spun away from him and dug out a pair of panties, listening to him laugh. "You asked for it, doll."

Lori snorted. "You're right. I just now realized that my going to Exposé was an invitation for you to jump my bones and tease me senseless."

She didn't hear him move. But he was there, behind her, brushing her hair aside and pressing a hot, open-mouthed kiss to her neck. His arms wrapped around her waist and he murmured, "I kept warning you. Not my fault you didn't pay attention to me."

Against her butt, she could feel the hard, thick length of his cock. After the past few hours, she shouldn't be the least bit interested. But her heart skipped a beat and her breathing got all shaky and shallow. Still, if she didn't eat something soon, she wouldn't be able to see straight. Or walk.

Well, walking was going to be interesting for the next little bit anyway. Every muscle in her legs screamed and between her thighs, Lori felt sore and achy.

"Food. Okay?" She tugged against his hands and turned to press a kiss to his mouth. "I need food and a shower."

"Spoilsport," he murmured. But he let go, his hands falling away. His hand came up and cupped her chin, lifting her face. He brushed a kiss against her lips. "I'm going home to grab some clothes. I'll be back."

Lori pushed up onto her toes and kissed him back. Before she pulled away, she nipped his lower lip. "You do that."

SIX

M ike had no more than grabbed a clean shirt from the dryer when he heard the front door open.

At the sound of Alex's deep voice, he swore. He headed out into the living room, about to tell Alex to get lost but then he saw his baby sister standing behind him.

Crossing over to her, he brushed a kiss against the top of her head and said, "Hey. What are you all up to?"

From the corner of his eye, he could see Alex studying him. Mike had grabbed a box of condoms from his bathroom and they were on the coffee table where he wouldn't forget them. And right where Alex could see them. Allie, too, if she ever stopped staring at her feet.

"We're going to catch a movie. I ran into Allie at the bookstore and, as always, she'd planned on spending the evening with her nose in a book. So I talked her into grabbing a bite to eat and a movie. We thought you might want to come," Alex said. A wicked grin lit his face. "But if you're busy . . . "

"Ah . . . sort of."

"Anybody I know?" His gaze drifted to the box of rubbers and Mike could feel blood rushing to his cheeks.

Casually, he dropped his clean shirt on the table, covering the black box just before Allie headed over to sit down on the couch. "If you've got plans, Mike, it's not a problem."

Mike narrowed his eyes at Alex, but before he could try to think of a polite way to get Allie and Alex to leave, the back door opened. "Hey, Mike. Do you want to . . . oh. Sorry." Lori stood in the doorway, her hair hanging in wet ringlets around her face. She wore a pair of brief white shorts and red T-shirt. Braless. Mike could see her nipples pressing against the cotton.

She stopped in her tracks when she saw Alex. Her cheeks flushed red. Mike wouldn't have been surprised if she turned tail and ran back to her house, but instead, she squared her shoulders and continued on inside. "Hi, Allie."

Allie smiled and went back to studying her short nails. "Hello, Lori."

Lori crossed the room and sat down beside Allie, casually drawing her knees to her chest. "How is nursing school going?"

Allie shrugged. "Two more years and I'll have my bachelor's."

"Still working at the nursing home?"

Finally, Allie looked up, a wry grin on her narrow face. "Where else?"

"Haven't seen you in a while, Lori." Alex stepped up, a devilish smile on his mouth. "Sorry if we interrupted something. I didn't know Mike had plans for the weekend. We were going to grab a movie. Why don't you all come with us?"

Mike tried to catch her eye but she wasn't looking at him.

Shit.

* * * * *

No wonder you've been keeping her to yourself."

Mike ignored Alex.

"So how serious is this?"

Mike finally turned to Alex and gave him a humorless smile. "Get a grip, Alex. I think we've had this discussion before. I'm not looking for long-term, pal. Not in the cards for me."

"Maybe you picked up a new game without realizing it," Alex drawled as the shuffled a little closer to the counter.

Mike just snorted. "Shit, Alex. Lori is a nice girl. With a capital N. I don't do nice. I don't even know how to handle nice. Hell, look at Allie. She's my kid sister and I can't be around her more than a few hours without pissing her off or saying something that hurts her."

Laughing, Alex replied, "You've been friends with Lori for four years. Hell, she's one of your best friends. I think you handle nice better than you think. Until you start letting it scare you."

"Scared. Scared of *what*? Allie? Lori?"

"Hell. You're scared of anything serious. You won't try for your lieutenant shield. You don't know how to handle your sister because you don't *want* to. She sees too much in you and you can't stand it. So yeah. Scared."

It made something twitch deep inside his gut, thinking about it. It was bullshit though. Plain bullshit. "You been watching *Dr. Phil* or something, Alex? That's the biggest load of crap I've heard all week."

For a minute, Alex just studied him, smiling a little. "So you're telling me there's not much going on between you two. She's not the reason you've been in a shitty mood for the past month."

"I've been in a shitty mood because we've had several cases go straight to hell and because it's been a shitty summer. I've been bored out of my mind, I'm tired, and I'm sick of the same old shit all the time. It has nothing to do with Lori," Mike snapped. Of course, he knew he was lying. Still didn't change the fact that he wasn't interested in long-term. This thing with Lori was just that. A *thing*.

It would end. Things would be like they used to be and—

"Well, if that's how it is, then cool. I gotta admit, I've been dying to get my hands on her. She's got an amazing ass. Tell me—"

Mike whirled on Alex and grabbed him by the front of his shirt, spinning them around and driving Alex back up against a black-and-white painted column. "Shut the hell up."

Alex was grinning, an amused little smirk that made Mike feel about as intelligent as an amoeba. Alex had been baiting him. Aware that people were staring at them, Mike slowly uncurled his fingers from Alex's shirt and backed off. "You're a twisted bastard, Alex. You know that?"

Instead of waiting for a reply, he fell back into line.

Alex joined him, still grinning like a fool. "You be sure to let me know when and if you feel like letting me join in. I wasn't kidding about her ass."

As Lori walked off to the bathroom, Alex stood up and said, "I'm going to grab a smoke."

Allie gave him a quick look before looking down at the floor. "Thought you were quitting."

He reached out and tugged on a lock of brown hair. "I'm working on quitting, Allie-cat. Right now, it's just in the planning-on-quitting-someday-soon stage."

"Someday." Allie snorted. "You know, if you keep putting it off, by the time someday rolls around, your taste buds are going to be shot and your teeth all yucky and yellow."

Mike smiled a little. It was weird hearing that dry, sardonic tone in her voice, even odder to see her look at Alex dead-on. She spent so much time staring at the ground, or beyond somebody's shoulder. Rarely dead-on. It was amazing that somebody who refused to really look at *anybody* could see so much.

Alex smiled. "Everybody has to have a hobby. Mine is procrastination." He headed outside and Mike shifted a little on the seat, hoping Lori would be out soon.

"I like her."

Mike glanced at Allie. "Who?"

Allie shrugged her thin shoulders and said, "Lori. She doesn't look at you like she's sizing you up and she doesn't treat me like some sort of reject."

"You're not a reject," Mike said automatically. Then he looked at her, wondering if he'd ever made her feel that way.

"I know that, Mike. But Lori is the only lady you've ever brought to your house for more than a few hours. And all your girlfriends? They acted like I was some sort of leper."

Mike winced. Okay, now that was true. They hadn't exactly been girlfriends, but there had been a few women who ended up getting dropped like yesterday's news because they treated Allie like crap.

"She's not my girlfriend, Allie. We're just . . . "

Allie grinned. It was a quick one, almost gone before it appeared. "Friends, huh. And that's why you keep giving Alex a 'drop dead' glare every time he gets a little too close."

SEVEN

"Are you okay?"

Mike lay sprawled on his belly, his face buried in Lori's scented sheets. They smelled of cherry blossoms and vanilla. The same scent he caught from her skin. It had been all over his body when he'd left her house earlier.

"I'm fine," he muttered.

Lori smoothed a hand down his back. She pressed her lips to his shoulder and pushed up onto her elbow. He could feel the ends of her hair brushing his skin. Part of him felt like he could lie there all night, just enjoying the touch of her hands on his back.

"You're awfully quiet."

But the soft, concerned sound of her voice kept intruding on his attempts to avoid thinking. Mike flipped onto his back and sat up, reaching down to cup his hand over her sex. She was still wet from him. He held her gaze as he pushed his finger inside. The slick, wet walls of her sex clasped him tightly.

"I'm horny," he muttered, leaning in and pressing a rough kiss to her lips. With his hands on her shoulders, he urged her to her back and ordered, "Flip over."

The minute she did, Mike slid his hands under her hips and pulled her up. He pushed into her without hesitation, groaning at the satin-slick feel of her pussy. He hadn't put a rubber on. He wasn't going to.

Lori didn't know it, but this was going to be their last time and he was going to feel her when she came. Feel *all* of her. "Mike . . . "

"I don't want to talk. I just want to fuck you."

He fell forward onto his hands, crushing her body into the mattress. He bit her shoulder and caught her hands in his, drawing them over her head. Blindly, he reached over and caught one of the scarves that Lori had draped around her bedpost. Tugging one free, he used it to tie her hand to one of the slats in the headboard. He tugged it to make sure it wasn't too tight. Then he grabbed another scarf and tied her other hand.

"Not exactly the black leather you're probably looking for, but this works," he whispered, trailing his fingers down her back.

Lori tugged on the scarves and then lifted her head, looking over her shoulder at him. Her eyes were big and dark, just a little nervous.

"Don't worry, baby. I promised I'd take it easy the first time," he said, forcing a smile that he didn't really feel inside. "Put your head down."

She did, hiding those soft blue eyes. Guilt knotted his belly and he almost pulled away. He couldn't though—proving just what a jackass he was. He was going to walk away, he knew it, but he was going to have her one more time.

And he did, hard and fast, dragging climax after climax from her. She felt so silky hot, the swollen tissues of her pussy clutching at his cock, tighter than a fist.

She came again and Mike gritted his teeth, holding desperately onto his control. As she collapsed limply onto the mattress, Mike pulled away. The brightly colored scarves were still tied to her wrists, securing her to the headboard.

"Not yet," he muttered as he again flipped her onto her back.

He crouched between her thighs, staring at her, etching the way she looked into his memory. Her mouth was parted, swollen and pink. Her breasts lifted and fell in a rapid rhythm as she tried to catch her breath. Her arms were stretched overhead, her wrists crossed now, the silky scarves tangled around her hands.

"You're beautiful, Lori." She was, so damn beautiful she made his heart ache. So damn sweet. Definitely not what he needed and he sure as hell wasn't what she needed or deserved.

He shoved the thoughts out of his mind. There'd be enough time to think about regrets and guilt later.

With focused intent, Mike sprawled between her thighs. He pushed them wide and lowered his mouth to her sex. He growled against her flesh and ordered, "Look at me."

Her lids lifted just barely and she stared at him as he pushed his tongue inside her snug, swollen folds. She shivered against him. He did it again and then he shifted his aim and licked her clitoris. Slowly, circling his tongue around the hard little nub. At the same time, he pushed two fingers inside her. She clenched down around him and screamed out his name.

She climaxed against his mouth and he pulled away. He angled her hips up with one hand and with the other he caught her behind her knee and pushed it to her chest. He thrust inside her, burrowing deep, until he could go no deeper. Turning his face to hers, he sought her mouth and kissed her, tangling his tongue with hers, trying to get as much of her taste as he could.

Sweat dripped from their bodies as he planted his palms on either side of her shoulders and pushed up. "Come for me," he whispered. He circled his hips in the cradle of hers then pulled out. A slow, shallow thrust then retreat, then a deep, hard thrust. He kept teasing her like that until she was panting and pleading with him.

He sank his weight back down atop her and eased his length completely inside, one inch at a time. "Come for me," he repeated. Then he started to shaft her, burying his cock completely before pulling back until he had nearly withdrawn. Two, three, four strokes.

On the fifth one, she exploded under him, her hips jerking convulsively. As she climaxed around him, he sank his teeth into her shoulder, biting down. As he exploded into her, she screamed and bucked under him.

Lori was so exhausted that she couldn't see straight. She could hardly move her legs, and her eyelids felt ridiculously heavy.

She wanted nothing more than to curl up against him and go to sleep, but Mike wasn't done. When he pulled away, she started to reach for him, but the scarves binding her wrists kept her from doing it.

"Untie me, Mike."

He stared at her, his eyes remote. He just shook his head silently and stood up. Her mouth was dry, but she wasn't sure if she was thirsty or nervous. He walked into the bathroom and Lori's eyes dropped to his ass. The hard, muscled curve had caught her eyes before and she wanted to touch him.

And she was going to, as soon as he untied her.

But the thought of what she wanted to do evaporated along with all other thoughts, when he came out of the bathroom.

He had a little glass bottle in his hand. It was massage oil. Lori had a weird feeling he wasn't planning on giving her a back rub with it.

"Roll over."

"Mike—"

He didn't let her finish. He covered her mouth with his, his tongue pushing inside. When he pulled away, she was breathless. By the time she caught her breath, Mike had rolled her onto her belly. Automatically, she pushed up on her knees, but with her wrists still trapped by the scarves, all she managed to do was stick her ass in the air.

Her face flamed and she started to roll back over, but Mike's hands caught her hips. "You said anything, Lori. Remember?" His voice was a husky whisper against her nape. He trailed his fingers down between her buttocks and pressed against the small opening there, a light, teasing touch.

"Remember?" he prodded again.

"Yes." Her voice came out in a terrified squeak as he touched her again. This time, his fingers were slick and wet with the oil. It was cool at first, but as he pushed inside the oil warmed.

Warmed, hell: she felt like it was scalding her—like he was scalding her. Stretching her. He pumped his fingers in and out, working more of the oil inside her with each caress.

"Are you ready?"

She felt him pressing against her, the head of his cock rounded and a hell of a lot bigger than his fingers. "No."

Mike just laughed a little. "Yeah, you are. You're so hot, you practically burn my hands." He smoothed one hand down her hip and held her still as he pushed against her.

Lori tried to pull away—pain speared through her as he pushed the head of his shaft inside, past the tight ring of muscle. "Don't pull away," he muttered. "That won't help. Push down on me."

Lori shook her head. She bit her lip to keep from crying out and wondered what in hell she had been thinking—damn it, women actually *liked* this?

His hand lifted and she thought for a second he would let her go. Instead, he slapped her ass. It was a hard, stinging smack and she jerked. "Push down!" His voice was commanding and instinctively she did as he said and pushed down.

As she did, he pushed inside. The pain didn't go away—it exploded into something else. Something caught between pleasure and pain, between heaven and hell. He pulled back and pushed inside again.

And again—each stroke made her burn a little hotter. He was stretching her, his cock thick and hard, carving through her tightness.

He slapped her again and Lori screamed out his name. He gripped both her hips now, holding her body still as he pulled out and thrust back inside her. Lori whimpered and shook underneath him.

She could feel the orgasm building inside her, something bigger, more exhilarating, more terrifying than anything she'd ever felt before. She shied away, squirming forward, trying to move away from him and the climax.

Mike wouldn't let her though. He slid one hand around, his fingers sliding over the slick, swollen flesh of her sex.

When he pressed down on her clit, the orgasm exploded

through her, taking her under like some big Goliath that swallowed her whole.

As she bucked, shuddered, and screamed her way through it, Mike came, his cock jerking inside her. She felt him come in a series of hot, wet pulses.

Blackness hovered around her, her vision graying out for just a second. She felt him moving, both his body and hers. Felt the tension around her wrists go free as he untied the scarves.

When she lifted her head, her vision had cleared. She turned to look at Mike, staring at him as he lay down beside her and took her in his arms.

"Go to sleep, Lori."

She tried to resist—she wanted to talk him. Ask him what was wrong. Wanted to ask . . .

But before she could say anything, sleep rushed up and claimed her.

Lori woke up alone.

It was Monday morning and she had to be at school in an hour. The students weren't due back for two weeks but Lori had a million things to do to get ready for the school year.

She couldn't force her body to move though.

Something had been wrong last night.

She'd known it when he rolled on top of her. She'd been uneasy even when he pushed inside her, but the feel of him, so thick, so hot, had distracted her. She was wet between her thighs, wet from herself and from him. He hadn't worn a rubber.

The only time all weekend.

She reached up and pushed her hair aside. Then she paused, staring at her wrist. There was a faint red mark on it. And on her other wrist. He hadn't tied her tightly, but she had jerked against the scarves hard enough, often enough, that she had faint little red marks on each wrist.

She would have smiled if she hadn't been so disturbed.

What had been wrong with Mike last night?

Finally, she sat up and headed into the shower, turning her back to the spray and letting it beat down on the tense muscles in her back. As she stood there, soaking up the steam, she brooded. Then she kicked herself about brooding.

So he'd been quiet last night. Big deal.

It wasn't like he was always a chatterbox.

Even as she worked herself around to not being so worried about it, she asked herself what it was. There was no relationship between them, right?

Maybe she had thought she'd felt a connection. Didn't mean Mike felt it. He hadn't implied anything like that and she had no reason to get her hopes up. The bad thing about sleeping with your best friend—you *knew* the person you were sleeping with. Like, *really* knew him. She knew that Mike had absolutely no interest in long-term relationships and marriage appealed to him about as much as getting an ice pick jabbed into his eye.

Unable to stop herself, Lori stood there analyzing every little thing that had happened since he'd left her house yesterday to change. That was when he'd started acting a little odd. A little more standoffish.

She snapped out of her daze and realized she was freezing. The water had gone cold and she hadn't even washed her hair. Shivering, she hurried through her shower and told herself to quit worrying. It had been an amazing weekend and even if that one weekend was all she got, that was fine.

He hadn't made any promises and Lori hadn't been looking for any.

Still, as she headed into her closet to find some clothes, she couldn't shake the vague sense of uneasiness.

I t only got worse.
    She saw Mike twice during the days that followed. He was avoiding her. There was no question about it. Each time was toward evening when he was heading home. The first time he headed inside without saying anything. The second time, she caught him as he was getting out of the car and he'd stood there for a few seconds and then given her some lame-ass excuse that he'd forgotten to do some paperwork.

She was rapidly approaching pissed by the time Friday rolled around. She wasn't sure who she was angry with though. Herself or Mike.

No, she really hadn't expected anything to come of the weekend they'd spent together, but she sure as hell hadn't expected him to start treating her like a pariah, either.

It was seven o'clock and Mike's driveway was empty. She tried to tell herself that it didn't matter. But there was an odd ache in her chest. Climbing from her car, she walked over to the picket fence that separated the properties. Lori wrapped her hands around two pickets and stood there, staring into nothingness as the ache in her chest spread.

"You screwed up, Lori," she told herself. She'd been attracted to Mike for a while, but she wasn't his type. He hadn't ever told her what type he did like, but Lori knew it wasn't her. She'd been okay with that because of their friendship.

Messing up that friendship was the last thing she had wanted. But it looked like that was exactly what had happened. Sex changed things. Even when the parties involved weren't looking for anything more.

"Yeah, but you were looking," Lori muttered and made herself deal with it. As much as she hated it, she had to be honest with herself. Yeah, part of her had been hoping for something more. And judging by the gaping, empty hole in her chest, it had been a *big* part.

S omething wrong?"

Alex glanced at the petite brunette across from him and just shook his head. "Just saw somebody I know." And it wasn't somebody he would have expected to see there, either.

Of course, she looked damn good. Good enough to eat, in fact, and Alex found himself wondering if he could talk Mike into sharing.

Lori Whitmore strolled along the outer edge of the dance floor, looking into the crowd, completely unaware of him. Which gave him the chance to admire the view. She wore something made of teal blue leather. It laced up between her breasts so that about an inch of skin showed between the lacings. It was short, ending just a few inches below her breasts, well above the waistband of the low-slung, wide-legged black pants. She wore a necklace of hammered silver and had pulled her butter-yellow curls into a high, loose ponytail.

"You know Lori?"

Alex looked at Grace with an arched brow. "How do you know her?"

Grace grinned. "We both work at Braxton Elementary."

With a chuckle, Alex said, "I wonder if the parents of this community have any idea the kind of perverts who are teaching their kids." He took a sip of his Coke, looking back at Lori. "She lives next door to my partner, Mike."

"Mike Ryan?" Grace had an odd tone in her voice as she looked at Lori. Her eyes were dark and she looked a little worried.

"Yeah. Mike won't admit it, but he's gone over on her."

Grace leaned back in her chair. "Apparently not too much. He's out in the maze."

Alex swore. Lori disappeared into the crowd and he stood up, craning his head to see. And he did, just in time to watch her slip out the back door.

She'd come here for a distraction, but it wasn't working.

In a desperate attempt to try to stop thinking about Mike for just a few minutes, she headed out into the maze. Part of her had been hoping to find Grace so she could maybe unload a little. Grace hadn't been at the bar or on the dance floor, though.

For some reason, Lori didn't expect she'd find her out in the maze—and if she did, she hoped she wouldn't die of embarrassment. She walked along the path, staring down at the stones or straight ahead. She didn't have to look to know what she wasn't seeing.

The breathy sighs and moans, the occasional bit of conversation. If you could call it that. Her face was red with embarrassment and Lori turned around. She was leaving. Maybe she'd go catch a movie or—

Not.

The first few seconds of what she saw didn't make any sense. She couldn't see anything of the woman except long legs wrapped in leather, a half naked back and yards of black curls. She was face down, literally, her face buried in Mike's crotch. As Lori watched, she lifted up and then slid back down.

Lori couldn't actually see what the bitch was doing, but she didn't have to.

She swallowed, feeling like somebody had dropped an anvil on her chest. She looked up at Mike's face and met his dark green eyes for the quickest of seconds. He stared at her with no expression on his face.

Without saying a word, she spun away and headed back toward the club as fast as she could.

It was a hell of a time to realize that she was a lot more involved in the thing with Mike than she'd realized.

She was in love with the son of a bitch.

Turning the corner, she plowed straight into a wide chest covered with plain white cotton. "Excuse me," she mumbled and tried to go around.

Big, hard hands came up and closed gently over her upper arms. "Hi, Lori."

Numb, she looked up and saw that it was Alex. Lamely, she replied, "Hi." Then she pulled away and went around him. He said her name, but she just kept walking.

Home. She wanted to go home.

* * * * *

W hat in hell are you doing?"
Braced against the high, curved back of the stone
bench, Mike looked up at Alex. "Do you mind? I'm busy." He looked back down at the woman kneeling in front of him and tried to remember her name. Buffy. Bambi. Something like that . . . he thought. The inky black of her curls spilled over her shoulders as she bobbed up and down.

Unless she had her mouth full, she annoyed the hell out of him. Called him "Master" and kept wanting him to call her "slave". But as long as she kept her mouth full . . .

Alex didn't walk away so Mike looked up at him. He ran a hand down what's-her-name's curls and fisted his hand at her nape, guiding her into a slower rhythm. "I'm not up for double play tonight, Alex. Go away."

"Apparently the only thing you're in the mood for is being an ass." He glared at the woman but she continued on, seemingly unaware.

But Mike couldn't focus on her very talented mouth when Alex continued to stand right there, glaring at him. He tugged on her curls, slowing her to a halt. She didn't pull away at first and Mike said, "Enough." He searched his brain for her name and finally remembered. "Kiki. Enough, Kiki. I need to talk to my buddy here."

She lifted her head and stared at him with neon blue eyes. She had to be wearing contacts. The blue looked too unnatural against her deep, olive-toned skin to be real. She batted heavily mascaraed lashes at him and then lowered her face to rub her cheek against his thigh. "I do not mind waiting, Master. Perhaps the two of you . . . " Her voice trailed off but he got the message.

Alex chuckled. "Master? Honey, go inside and find yourself somebody who'll appreciate you a little more."

She looked back at Mike but she wasn't going to find whatever she was looking for from him. "Go on inside, Kiki. Maybe some other time."

As she left, he stood up and adjusted himself, tugging up his zipper and buttoning his shirt before he sat back down. "Say whatever it is you want to say and then leave me the hell alone. I need a drink." Or five. Ten. However many it took to forget the wounded look he'd seen in Lori's eyes as she stood there staring at him.

Alex didn't waste any time. "What kind of idiot are you?"

"The thirsty kind. Anything else?" Mike replied.

"Lori was just out here. Please, tell me she didn't see you."

Mike shrugged. "She knows what happens out here. She doesn't want to see it then she shouldn't come out here."

"But did she know she was going to see *you* out here? And what in hell are you doing out here anyway? Did you two have a fight? I mean, even if you did, this definitely isn't the place to come. What in hell—"

Interrupting him, Mike snapped, "Damn it, what in hell are you, my mom? No, we didn't have a fight, but you're still assuming there's something going on between us and there's not. We spent one weekend together. We had sex. End of story."

"Except you don't turn into a mean bastard after a weekend of sex, pal. You've been a dick all week, but now I know why. You really *are* scared."

Mike rolled his eyes and stood up. "Don't start that shit again, Alex. I'm not relationship shy and I don't have any kind of commitment issues. Lori just isn't my type." He started to push past Alex but his partner lifted an arm, barring his way.

"She's not a type." Alex said it quietly. "She's a sweet lady."

Mike stilled. "I know that. She's a very sweet lady. She's a good girl and she expects the things out of life that good girls deserve. A husband, a family, a dog in the backyard. I can't give her that."

"Bullshit. You just don't want to try. Why are you so certain you can't have it? I mean, shit, look at what you came from. Your parents were so in love with each other it gave people cavities. If they hadn't died in the accident, they'd still be making moon eyes at each other."

Turning away, Mike rubbed his chest. It felt empty inside, hollow. Just like it did every time he thought of his folks. They'd been killed by a drunk driver years ago but it still felt like yesterday. He and Allie, they'd been lucky. Not only had they had two parents who loved them, their parents had loved each other as well.

But it had spoiled things for Mike a little. He didn't want to fall in love because he didn't want any less than his parents had had. And these days, that kind of relationship wasn't just rare, it was almost nonexistent.

"I know that, Alex. You think I wouldn't like to have what they had?"

"Most people would. You're not stupid, even if you have been acting it lately. I don't get it, Mike. This is your chance and you're throwing it away. You think you're going to have anything lasting with somebody like Bambi?"

"It's Kiki," Mike corrected absently. Then he shook his head. "No. I know that's not the kind of thing that lasts. That's why it's how I prefer things. Marriage, kids, the whole nine yards—can you see that working out for me? I'm a homicide detective and I spend my nights at a sex club. I don't see it."

"You're more than just a cop, buddy. That's why you're good at it. And you hardly ever come here anymore. You admitted it yourself, you're getting bored with it. So what's stopping you from going after Lori?"

"Just let it go." Mike shook his head and headed out of the alcove.

Alex caught his arm. "Not until I get an answer. I'm tired of you acting like an ass and—" His words ended abruptly and he just stood there, glaring at Mike.

"And what?"

Alex let go and turned away. Reaching, he rubbed at the back of his neck. Under the plain white T-shirt, his shoulders were stiff with tension.

"Alex, either say what you got to say or go away. I want a drink and I want it now," Mike snarled.

Alex turned around, his eyes dark and glittering. Unless Mike was mistaken, his face looked a little red too. Kind of flushed.

He realized why a few seconds later.

Alex was blushing. "You're my best friend, Mike. We've known each other our whole lives. I just want you to be happy." He gestured toward the club. "This . . . hell, this is just fun for us. It's not our lifestyle. You don't want some babe calling you Master and asking permission to go to the bathroom any more than I do."

Mike closed his eyes. No. That wasn't what he wanted. Up until a few weeks ago, Mike hadn't been sure what it was that he did want. He had a bad feeling, though, that he knew now.

He knew what. He knew who.

"Come on, man. This is your chance. Why are you trying to screw it up?"

Mike looked Alex square in the eye and said, "There's no trying to it. I already have screwed it up. I just . . . Hell."

Alex had been right.

Mike was scared. That's all there was to it. "Shit."

He opened his eyes and looked at Alex. "I think I really fucked things up."

Alex just shrugged a broad shoulder. "I dunno. Something tells me that Lori just might let this go, after she makes you crawl a little." A wide grin spread across his face. "Can I watch?"

Mike flipped him off and headed for the club.

Behind him, Alex asked, "Aren't you even going to say thank you?"

He spun around but kept walking. "Thanks."

Alex wagged his eyebrows. "I was thinking something a little more tangible than that. Like maybe let me have a taste of the pretty blonde thing . . . after a while. When she's done making you crawl and beg. See if she'd be willing to let me come play a little."

Mike just snarled at him.

As he spun back toward the club, he could hear Alex laughing behind him.

Lori was scared. Hell, screw scared. She was terrified.

She'd changed the locks after she'd kicked Dirk out, but that hadn't kept him out. The shattered glass and the rock on the kitchen floor made it pretty clear how he had gotten inside, too.

He stared at her with a wild, half manic look in his gray eyes and something about that look made her skin crawl. He didn't look like he had shaved in a week and his clothes were wrinkled, his hair a mess. Considering that Dirk was the ultimate metro-sexual, it wasn't just surprising to see him that way.

It was downright disturbing.

"I saw you."

When he spoke, his voice was soft, almost whisper quiet. No reason for it to terrify her. But it did.

"Saw me where, Dirk?" Her cell phone was in her purse. If she could get to it . . .

He laughed and took a step toward her, then another. She started to back away but he didn't move any closer. Instead, he started circling her. "With him. I've been watching you. You've been going to that club." He nodded a little. "That's my fault. I should have listened when you said you wanted to go. You want to get fucked and let other people watch, hey, why not? But you had to fuck *him?*"

Dread curdled in her belly. He had been watching her? And he'd seen her with Mike. It hadn't occurred to her that Dirk would go all stalker crazy on her, but apparently that was exactly what had happened. And if he had gone and gotten obsessive, seeing her with Mike was *not* a good thing.

Dirk couldn't stand Mike. Lori had always suspected that Mike intimidated the hell out of Dirk, made him feel inadequate.

He stopped in his tracks, staring out the bay window. It faced toward the back, but the angled side windows let her see the back half of Mike's house and that was where Dirk was looking. "Of all the guys, you had to pick him."

While he had his back to her, Lori carefully slid her hand in her purse and grabbed her phone. He turned to her and she tucked her hand behind her back, hiding the phone from his view.

"Why him, Lori?" he asked, his voice soft and silky. "Of all the guys, you had to sleep with Mike. Had to let him touch you. Why did you do that?"

She lied. What the hell else could she do? Dirk had gone over the deep end and Lori wasn't planning on letting him take her with him. "I'm sorry, Dirk. I wasn't thinking," she said. It wasn't too hard to sound upset, considering she was absolutely terrified. He didn't need to know it was fear making her voice so shaky, right? "I was just so hurt. So lonely . . . "

Dirk nodded like he understood. "Were you missing me, baby?" he murmured, moving a little closer.

As he did, Lori realized it wasn't shaving he had been neglecting. He smelled like he hadn't taken a bath in a week. She started to breathe shallowly through her mouth so she wouldn't take in so much of the sour scent of his body.

"Did you miss me?" he asked again.

"Every day." Okay, squeezing that lie out hadn't been easy. When he stepped even closer, warning sirens started to screech in her head. Lori spun away from him and went to the table. She'd never been the best actress but she sat down and buried her face in her arms and started to wail. "I just missed you so much. But after what you did . . . "

He made shushing sounds and she flipped open the phone, hoping she had it hidden well enough. With her hair falling in her face and her other arm up, she just might . . .

"So that's why you went to Mike."

Lori wailed a little louder and hoped it covered the sounds as she keyed in 911. His hand touched her between the shoulder blades and he rubbed her back in soothing, slow strokes. "I knew you were just trying to punish me." He moved away and she heard a cabinet open, heard the water running.

She breathed out a sigh and carefully sat up, keeping the phone in her hand. From the corner of her eye, she could see him filling a glass with water and she tucked her hand under the table.

She tried to muffle the sound with her hand, but the tinny . . . *"911. What is your emergency . . . "* was loud and clear.

Dirk turned around and stared at her, his eyes narrowed down to slits. As he lunged for her, she jumped up from the table and put it between them. "Stupid bitch! Lying whore!"

"You don't really think I'd take you back, do you?" she said, sneering at him. "You're pathetic."

"Shut *up!*" he bellowed. He feinted to the left and Lori moved with him, keeping the table between them, not letting him force her to move anywhere she didn't want.

She could still hear the operator's voice coming from the phone in her hand. Keeping Dirk in her sights, she lifted it up and said, "I've got an intruder." She barely managed to recite her address before he came over the table at her. She backpedaled and slammed into the island. He caught there, pinning her up against it.

"You're going to pay for that, Lori," he panted, struggling to pin her hands. Lori fought back, fighting to get just a little bit of leverage. She brought her foot up and slammed the heel of her boot onto his foot, grinding down. He yelped and one hand loosened enough that she was able to jerk her arm free. Stiffening her fingers, she jabbed them into his throat.

He fell back, choking for air and Lori scrambled away. She nearly made it to the front door when he caught her. She went down struggling and as he flipped her over, she jerked her knee up, catching him square in the balls. "The police are coming, Dirk. You need to get lost."

His eyes were wild. His face was pale and he could hardly breathe, but he pinned her down, his knees pressing into her upper arms to keep her trapped against the floor. He reached down, closing his hands around her throat. "You're mine, Lori. If I can't have you . . ."

She struggled to breathe as pain exploded through her. His fingers got tighter and tighter and she kicked, but he had her pinned a little too well. She could feel it, the strength draining out of her, the blackness growing. Her lungs threatened to burst from the pressure and still she couldn't get a breath in.

As everything went completely black, she heard a crash.

EIGHT

For the rest of his life, he was going to see it. Dirk on top of Lori, his hands choking the life out of her.

When the 911 call had come through, he had been almost home. Terror had turned his blood to ice and he had put the gas pedal to the floor, keeping it there until he pulled into Lori's yard. Literally. He had taken out the white picket fence and destroyed several of her flower beds as he practically drove his car through the front of her house.

He'd buy her new flowers. Hell, he'd buy her an entire warehouse of them, so long as she lived.

Alex had shown up at the hospital just as the security guards were trying to drag Mike from the treatment room. How the hell Alex knew already, Mike didn't know. Didn't care. He'd almost popped Alex in the mouth because he was helping the security guards drag him away.

"Come on, Mike. Let them help her . . . " Those words finally penetrated and Mike had let Alex guide him out. That had been nearly thirty minutes ago. Although nurses came and went from the curtained-off room, not one of them had approached.

Finally, the curtain was pushed back and Mike stood up. His legs felt leaden and he was pretty damn sure he was going to choke if he had to say anything. The knot in his chest was so damn huge, he could hardly breathe.

Fortunately, he didn't have to say anything.

She was young, pretty and looked entirely too perky for Mike's peace of mind, and she smiled at him. "She's going to be fine. There's been some trauma to her throat and she was without oxygen for a few minutes . . . "

Mike knew that. He had been doing CPR when the ambulance got there. She hadn't been breathing . . .

"We're going to have to keep her overnight. I think she's got a few broken ribs, either from the attack or the emergency CPR, I'm not sure. We're going to X-ray . . . "

Nothing else she said made sense. Mike stopped listening. He moved past the doctor, aware that she was following him, that she was still speaking, but none of it mattered.

What mattered lay in the bed in front of him. Her face was pale, but unmarked. Apparently, Dirk hadn't been interested in beating on her, just killing her. The evidence of that lay in hideous, ugly red bruises that ringed her pale throat.

As he sat down on the stool beside her stretcher, her eyes opened. She opened her mouth to talk but all that came out was a weird, garbled sound. He reached up and touched her lips. "Don't try to talk. Your throat's going to hurt for a little while."

She stared at him at him for a moment and then her lids drooped. Within a few seconds, she was fast asleep.

"We gave her some pain medicine. There's no head trauma, no cuts, no lacerations. Really, she's incredibly lucky. Aside from her ribs and the trauma to her throat, she's unharmed."

Mike looked over his shoulder at her and rasped, "You call this lucky?"

The doctor gave him a sad little smile and suddenly she didn't look so young and perky. Her hazel eyes looked incredibly old as she murmured, "Yes. She's alive. All of her injuries will heal. You all got to her before he . . . " Her voice trailed off but Mike knew what it was that went unsaid.

Before Morrigan could have killed her, raped her, or both.

She turned and left but before the curtain swung back into place, a dark hand caught it. Alex stepped inside. He looked at Lori for a second and then looked at Mike.

"You okay, man?"

"No." Mike lowered his head to the stretcher. He reached up with one hand and sought Lori's, linking their fingers and pressing his palm to hers. "No, I'm not."

She woke up surrounded by flowers.

On the table nearest her bed, there was a huge crystal vase. It sparkled in the light filtering through the blinds. It held roses, dozens of them. Each one a deep, perfect shade of red.

She reached up and touched her fingers to one of the petals.

"You're awake."

Lori rolled her head on the pillow, too damn tired to lift it. She found herself practically nose-to-nose with Mike. He had huge bags under his eyes, his hair was standing on end and he looked like he had aged ten years.

"You look awful," she said baldly. Her throat hurt like fire when she spoke and she reached up, touching it with her fingers. Even that light touch hurt.

"Don't try to talk," he murmured. He reached up and caught her hand, drawing it away from her throat. "It's going to be a day or two before you can speak without it hurting so much."

Mike stared at her, his eyes focused, intent. "God, I'm so sorry." His eyes dropped down and she knew he was staring at her throat.

Ignoring his order that she not speak, she asked, "How bad is it?"

He cocked a brow. "Don't talk." Then he reached up and gently touched one finger to her neck. "Bruised. Very ugly and bruised. But it will be okay. Do you remember?"

Lori nodded silently. She wanted to say something. But she wasn't sure what. *It's a good thing I didn't marry him. How did I get out of there alive?* Those were the questions she *should* be asking.

Instead, she found herself wanting to yell at him about the bimbo brunette who had been giving him a blow job. She wanted to gouge the woman's eyes out. And then either slap Mike or jump him.

Not very normal reactions for somebody who had been nearly choked to death, she was sure.

So she focused on one thing she really did need to know. "Dirk?"

His eyes fell away. "He's dead."

Her eyes widened. "How?"

"Later. When you feel better. Now will you stop talking?" he asked with a pained expression. "The sound of your voice makes *my* throat hurt."

Lori nodded. "After you tell me one thing."

Mike scowled a little. "What?"

"If you were going to start pretending I didn't exist after . . ."

Her voice trailed off. *After a weekend of wonderful sex.* Lamely, she just left it at that. "Why did you even bother? We were friends."

"Lori, this isn't a good time to talk about it." His eyes were flat and unreadable. "You don't know how badly you were hurt."

"Mike—"

His voice rose. "Didn't you hear me? You weren't breathing!" He was shouting by the time he finished, his face tight with fury. He closed his eyes and she watched him battle the rage. His voice was a little softer when he continued, "You weren't breathing. Do you have any idea how much that scared me, seeing you there like that?"

"Seeing me . . . You found me?"

He nodded curtly. "I had left the club to come and find you when I heard the 911 call on my radio. I was nearly home. And still almost didn't make it in time. You were lying on the floor and he . . . "

He closed his eyes, rubbed them, as if he could wipe the memories away. "He was choking you. He pulled a knife. He must have grabbed it out of your kitchen. If he had used it instead of his hands, you wouldn't be here."

"Oh, God." Nausea roiled in her belly and she clapped a hand over her mouth. If she threw up . . .

Mike was there, rubbing her back with a gentle hand. "You don't need to hear about this right now," he said.

Lori leaned into him, her mind whirling as it pieced things together. He hadn't said it, but Lori knew. Mike had killed Dirk. She had been engaged to the man for nearly a year, with him for three. But all she felt was relief and some distant sort of regret. She wasn't really even angry, although she suspected she would be eventually.

"Why were you coming to look for me?" she asked. Every word felt like she was pushing raw glass through her throat, but she had to know.

Mike sighed. "You must enjoy having your throat hurt like that."

"I just need to know."

He shifted around, turning so that he sat on the edge of the bed, facing her. "To tell you I was sorry. I knew you were in the maze. And I'm sorry. But also, for the past week. I've been a bastard."

"Why? I mean, it's not like I was expecting rose petals and a diamond ring."

She stared at him as he reached down and took her hand, rubbing the back with his thumb. "I know. The problem is, part of me wanted just that."

Her jaw dropped open. She probably looked like an idiot, lying there staring at Mike with her mouth hanging open but she just couldn't help it. He reached up and pressed his finger against her chin, closing her mouth. "Don't look at me like that."

"What are you talking about?"

Instead of answering right away, Mike leaned over and pulled one of the roses from the vase. He stared at it intently as he started to pluck the satiny petals off. He dropped each one on the sheets that covered her lap. "I'm not much into romance. Never have been. That probably won't change. But you're the only woman I've ever met who made me want to give her roses, Lori. You're the only one who's ever made me want a little something more. And it scares the hell out of me. I don't react well to being scared."

His gaze lifted and Lori felt her heart stutter to a stop at the emotions she saw there. "If last weekend was just a thing for you, that's fine. I'll deal with it. But if . . . Well, maybe it meant a little more and that maybe, well . . . I mean, if I haven't totally fucked it up with what happened at Exposé, maybe we could . . . "

How cute. A smile spread across her face, and if it wouldn't have hurt so much she would have laughed. As he fumbled for the words, she couldn't help but think how damn cute it was, seeing him look so damn awkward.

Finally, though, she leaned in and pressed her lips to his. It was either kiss him or let him try to explain for the next thirty minutes. She'd rather kiss him.

Pulling back, Lori reached up and cupped his cheek. "Yeah. Maybe we could . . . "

DROP DEAD
SEXY

Elisa Adams

ONE

"If you could do anything in bed with a woman, what would it be?"

The keys slid from Nathan's hand and hit the ground with a clang of metal. His mouth went dry and his cock, never completely dormant around his drop-dead sexy neighbor, went rock-hard. A hundred ideas raced through his mind, half of which Joy had probably never even heard of. And the other half . . . *Jesus Christ.* If he told her what he wanted to do to a woman—to *her*—in bed, she'd never speak to him again. "Excuse me? Why would you even ask me that?"

"I'm just curious."

The sparkle in her blue eyes told him there was more to her question than simple curiosity. Seduction wasn't on her mind either, at least he didn't think so, given the pajama shorts and tank top she wore and the messy ponytail she'd thrown her curly, auburn hair into. Thank God for that. Most nights he simply avoided her, but tonight she'd managed to sneak up on him as he was coming home, throwing herself in his path and asking such an outrageous question that he couldn't help but be intrigued.

He slumped against the wall and crossed his arms over his chest, trying to think of a way to get rid of her. Intrigued or not, answering her question would only lead to problems he'd rather avoid. A sweet, innocent woman like his neighbor would run in the other direction if she knew what he'd want to do with a woman in bed. She wouldn't want to get caught up with someone like him. Would never understand his unusual needs. No matter how cute Joy was, she wasn't his type.

"That's an odd thing to be curious about." Though for her, he knew it wasn't. Every time they spoke, she had some sort of question for him. He supposed it went with the territory of living across the hall from a freelance journalist. The questions in the past had been simple, if not a little annoying, but they'd never even skirted the issue of sex until tonight. Tonight she'd changed the rules, and his body had sat up and taken notice in a big way. "What's really going on? Is this for work?"

She started to shake her head but then stopped and bit her lip. "Okay, so it's for work. Is that a crime?"

A sliver of disappointment worked its way into his mind, but he pushed it away. Why should he be irritated that she wasn't interested in him, just interested in picking his brain? He shouldn't be, but for some illogical reason he was. "Go home, Joy."

"Answer my question first." Her eyes narrowed and she raised her chin, and Nathan almost laughed. There was nothing tough about Joy Baker, no matter how much she tried to pretend there was. She was all sweetness and innocence wrapped up in a short, curvy package. The woman probably couldn't even kill a spider if she found one in her apartment. She could play tough all she wanted, but he wasn't buying it for a second.

"It's not a crime, but it could be dangerous to go around asking men you barely know what they like to do to women in bed." He lowered his voice to a near whisper. "You might end up getting more than you bargained for."

"Maybe I can handle a lot more than you think."

The thought made him swallow hard. So much for trying to chase her away. Now all he could think about was shoving her up against the wall, peeling off those insubstantial shorts and sinking his cock deep into her pussy.

Not that it would ever happen. In his experience, there were two types of people in the world when it came to sex—those who were adventurous and those who weren't. Joy looked like a straight-up missionary type of woman. The kind who tolerated sex and then rolled over and went to sleep. No way in hell could he deal with that, no matter how tempting those full lips were.

With a muttered curse, he bent and scooped his keys off the ground. He stood and unlocked the apartment door, suddenly needing to put some distance between them. A lot of distance. If he kept looking at her wearing next to nothing, breathing in her sweet scent of apples and flowers and warm, soft woman, he might just give her something she wasn't even asking for.

"Good night, Joy. Go home and get some sleep."

"Wait a second." Her fingers grasped the short sleeve of his T-shirt and she gave it a little tug. He tried to shake off the warmth that spread from his arm to all points in his body, but he couldn't quite manage it. "Can you please just give me five minutes of your time? I need your help."

Nathan leaned in and pressed his forehead to the doorjamb. Why now, of all times? With his family pushing him to do some-thing he had no interest in, did she have to start asking provocative questions? They wanted him to find a nice woman and settle down. If his mother found out about Joy and his attraction to her, she'd never leave either of them alone. Now, with *settling down* the furthest thing from his mind, it wasn't the time to be getting involved with any woman, let alone one right across the hall.

"Shouldn't you be asleep?"

Images of Joy in bed flashed through his mind, and they didn't help his current situation. Joy naked, writhing on his sheets. Screaming his name as he—

Hell no. He needed to get inside before they both ended up in a heap of trouble.

"I'm writing an article for a women's magazine, and I've been researching. I heard you walking down the hall, and I thought having a live interview subject would be better than trying to weed through all the crap on the Internet."

He shook his head back and forth against the cool wood. "You're writing about what men want in bed?"

If so, that was an easy answer. He wanted Joy, completely bared to him, body and soul. On his bed, his couch, even on his fucking kitchen table. At this point, he wasn't in any state to be picky.

"The article is about how a woman can make her man's fantasies come true. Since I don't have a man of my own right now, I can't ask him what he'd want. I figured you, of all people, would understand sexual fantasies."

Now wait a minute. What the hell was that supposed to mean? He turned around, his eyes narrowed. "Excuse me?"

Her shrug was casual enough, but the smug smile on her face told him she knew she'd gotten to him. "Just that I see you with a different woman every weekend."

"Just because I bring them here doesn't mean I sleep with them." *And even if I do, it's none of your business.* His family bothered him enough about his revolving girlfriends. Was there something wrong with a guy wanting to have a little fun before he was forced to settle down?

"It's always the middle of the night, and they're always all over you. Tell me you don't take them to bed."

The challenge written in her eyes brought a smile to his face. She'd noticed. That meant she'd been watching him as much as he'd been watching her. "Are you spying on me?"

"Of course not." She wrinkled her nose. "I'm a night person, usually awake watching TV when you bring your giggly, obnoxious girlfriends down the hallway. The walls around here are so thin I can practically hear what they're saying when they whisper in your ear."

Was that a hint of jealousy he detected in her voice? Nah. Couldn't be. She'd been avoiding him, and he'd been avoiding her.

Why had he been doing that again?

Because she wasn't. His. Type.

And if he repeated that a few thousand times, he might actually start to believe it. She *was* his type. *Exactly* his type, and his body had known it before his mind. But he'd be damned if he was going to be forced into something he wasn't ready for just because of some stupid tradition. He and his family had opposing views on lifetime commitment—they were all for it, and he preferred to pretend it didn't exist.

He blew out a breath. The situation was quickly moving into territory he'd rather not explore. At least not yet. In the two months since he'd moved in across the hall from her, they'd probably spoken a total of a hundred words to each other. This was the longest conversation they'd had to date, and yet he'd never really been able to get her off his mind. It was because he was a fucking fool, believing he could live across the hall from her, catch her scent in the air every day and not go out of his goddamned mind.

With a heavy sigh, he pushed away from the doorjamb. "Are you calling me a slut, Miss Baker?"

Humor sparked in her eyes. She raised her eyebrows but said nothing.

"And you think I'm willing to divulge my deepest, most secret fantasies to you so you can use them in some fluffy article for a *women's* magazine?"

"It would be anonymous. I wouldn't use your name or any identifying details. Just the fantasies you're willing to share. I'm not writing erotica. It's just an article. What's the harm in answering a couple of stupid questions?"

The questions posed no problem. It was what they might lead to that bothered him. "Okay. You want to ask questions, who am I to stop you?"

"You'll help me?"

He nodded. As if she'd given him any choice. He'd help, but it would come with a price. He'd kept his distance from her. Until tonight. Now she wanted to change the way their relationship—or lack thereof—worked, and he had a feeling nothing he could say would dissuade her. He'd been a gentleman. Until now. The second she walked over the threshold into his apartment, all bets were off. "Better get inside quick, before I change my mind."

If he could keep his hands off her for five minutes, they'd both be lucky. At this rate, three minutes without touching her would be a freakin' miracle.

After only a second's hesitation, she scooted inside and he followed, closing the door behind them. He switched on the light by the door and turned to face her. The second her gaze snagged his, the room seemed to shrink to the size of a postage stamp. He couldn't tear his eyes away, and each second passed like an eternity.

He swallowed against the dryness in his throat. If he hadn't been sure before, he was now. He was a goner.

Joy glanced away, her gaze taking in his plain, white-walled apartment, and he cleared his throat. "You want a beer or something?"

"No, thanks. I don't drink."

"Water? Coffee?"

"Thanks anyway. I'm all set. Nervous about something?"

Nervous? No. Horny and ready to jump all over her was more like it. That and a few other things he wouldn't even allow himself to think about. It would be best to keep his thoughts on track for now or risk spilling his whole story. She'd have to know soon, but not yet. If he told her now, she'd think he was some kind of deranged stalker.

Time to focus on the more immediate matter of Joy's question. What he would want to do with a woman in bed.

What the hell did she want from him, anyway? Women didn't really want to know about men's fantasies, did they? Of course not. They wanted a glazed-over, sweetened version that wouldn't make them feel guilty in the morning. Why would Joy be any different?

"I have nothing to be nervous about. I'm just trying to be a good host." A host to a woman he wanted out of his apartment and out of his mind before she caused permanent damage to his carefully ordered life.

She laughed then—a rich, husky sound that sent heat spiraling through his gut. It settled in his cock and made him harder than before. *Shit.* Why wouldn't she just go home? Just talking about his fantasies was going to make him think of all the things he wanted to do to her. Things she would never let him do.

Fuck this. Keeping his distance wasn't working. Maybe scaring her off would send her packing and he could get on with his life. If not, they both had to live with the consequences.

"I could tell you all about my fantasies," he started, moving across the carpet toward her. "But I'd rather show you. Firsthand experience is always the best way to learn."

TWO

Joy's jaw dropped. Was he kidding? Her gaze flew to his jeans and the impressive bulge she found there. Her panties went damp. Okay, so he wasn't kidding. Go figure. He'd never hinted at being interested before. She'd always thought her complete and total lust for the guy was one-sided, but apparently she'd been wrong.

She licked her lips and took a deep breath, trying to calm her suddenly raging hormones. She hadn't anticipated this. This was *so* not a place she wanted to be tonight. All she'd wanted was to finish her article. Well, almost all . . . Still, deadlines needed to come before men, no matter how tempting the man was. "Not a good idea. You're really not my type."

It was a total lie, but she'd never admit it to the man.

"How do you know that? We've barely even spoken before."

"I just want to ask you a few questions. I'm not looking for a one-night stand."

"So ask." He took a step closer and then another until he stood only a few inches away. Her whole body took notice. Her fingers itched to thread through all that dark hair. She wanted to feel him. Wanted to taste him. Did he really expect her to ask him questions now, with him standing so close?

As if she could even form a coherent thought with so much testosterone filling the air around them. This was exactly why she normally avoided men like Nathan Halloran—they were more trouble than they were worth. It would be best to stick to the subject for her article tonight: men's fantasies and how women can fulfill them.

Damned if she didn't want to fulfill all of his, right that second.

"Okay, answer my first question. The one I asked right before you dropped your keys."

"What would I want to do with a woman in bed? Sweetheart, most of my fantasies don't even involve a bed. I can think of a lot of other places where I'd rather have fun."

Her panties dampened even more and her nipples poked against the soft fabric of the tank top. Her body swayed toward him and if she hadn't caught herself in time, she would have ended up draped against that hard chest. What had she gotten herself into? Thinking Nathan could help her with her research might have been a bit of a mistake. Suddenly a simple interview wasn't going to work for her anymore. Now that he'd made the suggestion to show her, she wanted to find out his fantasies in a much more physical manner. "Would you care to elaborate?"

"The weather is nice this time of year." He glanced toward the sliding door leading out onto the small balcony identical to hers. "Don't you think?"

"You like to do it outside? In *public*?"

"Sometimes. It mixes things up a little so life doesn't get boring."

She didn't care for boring, but she couldn't do something that would get her arrested either. *That* would lead to too many questions she didn't want to answer. "I would hardly think sleeping with a different person every Friday night would get boring."

"Trust me. It does."

The sincerity in his tone resonated somewhere inside her. She didn't have to take his word for it. She knew. She'd sworn off men—and sex—for that very reason months ago. Up until tonight, she hadn't even missed it. Much.

Instead of prying into his personal life, she made one last attempt to keep things as professional as they could be, given that she'd ambushed him in his hallway minutes earlier. "Talk to me, Nathan. Tell me what it is that men *really* want."

"Are you sure you want the answer to that?"

"My career might depend on it." This article was big. Huge. Or at least it had the potential to be. It could make or break her budding career and at this stage in her life, the thought of searching for a job in another field made her head ache. Been there, done that, had the lousy paycheck stubs to prove it.

Nathan laughed. The deep sound of it made her toes curl and she delighted in the little shiver that ran through her. He wasn't her type, and that fact drew her to him even more. She usually preferred sleek, stylish men in designer suits. Polished men. Nathan was far from polished and at first she'd wondered what the bevy of women he brought home saw in him, but it wasn't long before she'd figured it out. There was something about him that made it impossible to look away. His features were a little rough, his appearance a little less than perfect, but all in all, the package was so unbelievably sexy that she couldn't help but be drawn in.

"Okay. What men really want." His smile was nothing short of sinful. "Just remember, you asked for it. Most men need visual stimulation. They like to see a woman in sexy lingerie. Like to see her doing sexy things. Dancing or stripping, or even eating can be a huge turn-on if she's making it sexy. Words aren't really important most of the time. I know you don't want to hear this, but emotions usually aren't either. The visuals are."

"So you don't like a woman to talk dirty to you?" The question was out before she could stop it. She gave herself a mental kick in the butt for egging him on. She was there for research, not to get laid, no matter how much the latter appealed to her deprived body.

"I didn't say that at all. I just said it wasn't a necessity. Now *this* is another story." He flicked the strap of her tank top and it slid off her shoulder, revealing the top curve of her breast. His gaze dropped down and lingered, heat flashing in his eyes. "Walking into a room and seeing you like this would get me hard in about two seconds."

She put the strap back in place, her face flaming. Up until that moment, she'd forgotten that she'd run out of her apartment in her pajamas. She'd been so eager to talk to him that she hadn't even realized how indecent she must look. At least she had shorts on this time. Most nights she slept in just a tank top and under-wear. "Oh really."

She tried to keep her tone casual, but the look in his eyes when he raised his gaze back to hers told her she'd failed.

"A lot of men like women who are bold in bed, who aren't afraid to tell a man what they want. But at the same time, it can be a huge turn-on if a woman lets the man dictate what's going to happen and when. If she gives herself over to him and lets him take care of her pleasure." A sensual smile stretched his lips. "What do you want, Joy? What do *you* like in bed?"

Crap. At the moment, she didn't care. Anything he wanted would be fine. She just wanted something to ease the ache that had started the second Nathan had dragged her into his apartment. "Uh . . . "

"Do you like the man you're with to decide for you? To take charge?"

Not usually, but something about Nathan made that idea seem like the best one she'd heard in a long time. She opened her mouth to deny his claim, but nothing came out.

"What's the matter? Aren't you going to answer me?"

He stepped closer and reached out to grasp a strand of her hair. Standing this close to him, she got her first good look at his eyes. They were green. A deep, mossy color threaded with golden flecks. His hair was dark, the color of espresso, and it hung to his shoulders. Up until she stood so close to him, she hadn't realized how tall he was. Probably around six foot two, though almost all men looked tall from where she stood at five foot three.

"This isn't about what I want."

"Isn't it?" He gave the strand of hair a tug and she moved forward, her bare toes bumping into his boots. Nathan laughed and dropped her hair, his finger trailing down the side of her cheek to her neck. Joy swallowed hard and tried to back away, but his free hand grasped her arm and held her near him while he continued his exploration.

His finger dipped lower, down the side of her neck, before he brought it down and circled her nipple through the fabric of her top. The nub of flesh went even harder and she let out a little sound of surprise.

"No. This is about what *men* want. If it was about me, I wouldn't have needed to bother you with questions."

"Oh really?" He leaned in and nipped at her neck, sending a riot of sensation through her core. The feel of the man's teeth against her skin drove her wild. Almost out of their own volition, her hands came up and grabbed his shoulders, her fingers digging into the soft material of his shirt. "Is that all this is about? An article?"

Not even close. "Well, it's certainly not your stellar charms."

That got another laugh out of him. "You haven't been interested, even a little bit?" His tongue grazed the side of her neck and her fingers tightened against his arms. "'Cause I've been interested in you."

"Why didn't you ever say anything?"

"You're not my type." His mouth closed over her earlobe and he nibbled on the sensitive flesh.

A tremor raced through her pussy. Her back arched. "What exactly is your type?"

Her lobe left his mouth with a pop and he stood up, dislodging her hands from his shoulders as he moved a few inches away from her. He stared at her for a long time, eyes narrowed, before he spoke in a low whisper. "It's hard to explain. I just know that you're not it. But at the same time, something makes me think you are."

"That makes no sense."

"Tell me about it." He shook his head and seemed to shake off the confusion filling his gaze at the same time. When he looked at her again, it was with nothing but heat and lust and something undefined that made her pussy quiver again. He moved back and flopped onto the couch, his legs stretched out in front of him and his hands clasped behind his head. "Take off your shirt, sweetheart."

Sweetheart? Was he kidding? "I'm not one of your fan club."

A short chuckle followed her denial. "I'm aware of that. Actually, I'm very aware of everything about you. Take off your shirt and let me see those amazing breasts."

The deep, hypnotic quality in his voice sent a shiver through her. Her body begged for her to listen to him, to do as he asked in hopes of getting a little relief from the frustration she'd felt for so long. If anyone could relieve the bone-deep boredom that had settled in, it was Nathan and this little game he was playing. If she had to admit the truth, she'd wanted him for too long to deny herself the pleasure of finally having him. He wanted an obedient woman? Fine. She could manage that. For a little while. Her turn would come next.

"Afraid of something?" The taunting in his voice prodded her to move. Her fingers found the hem of her tank top and she pulled it over her head. A second later, the soft material dropped to the floor at her feet.

Nathan said nothing, but his eyes darkened even more. He licked his lips.

Goose bumps broke out over her skin, and they had nothing to do with a chill in the air. His scrutiny seemed to go on forever. The intensity in his gaze made her every muscle clench tight. Her nipples were so hard they ached.

"Touch them for me," he said in a low growl. "I want to watch you play with your nipples."

Her hands shaking, she brought them up and cupped her breasts. She flicked her thumbs across her nipples and moaned from the sparks the contact ignited.

"Pinch them," he told her.

"Why don't you?"

A deep chuckle vibrated through the room. "Come over here and I will."

When she didn't move, he raised his eyebrows. "Come over here and sit in my lap, Joy."

Her gaze dropped down to his lap and the bulge of his cock straining against his jeans. She licked her lips. He didn't have to ask her twice. She walked over to the couch, straddled his legs and lowered herself down until her pussy rested against that bulge. The urge to rub herself against him was strong, but she held back, wanting to see what Nathan had in mind.

She expected him to touch the breasts he'd been staring at since she'd stripped off her top, but he didn't. Instead he leaned in and captured her lips.

The kiss was deep, possessive, his tongue probing the recesses of her mouth. His fingers threaded through her hair and he tilted her head to deepen the kiss. She moaned against his lips. It had been forever since someone had kissed her like that. Like she was the only woman in the world he'd ever wanted.

Heat started low in her stomach and spiraled out to her limbs. Her lips tingled. Her fingers dug into his shoulders as she held on tight, reveling in every sensation he stirred inside her.

Her back arched, forcing her bare breasts against his chest. Her nipples rubbed against the fabric of his shirt and she cried out, the sensations almost too much to take. She needed so much more than a kiss. Needed it soon.

He broke the contact, trailing his tongue down her neck until he reached her breasts. In the next second, his hands cupped her breasts and he plumped them together. He leaned down and bit one of her nipples.

A gasp caught in her throat. "What are you doing?"

"Let me worry about that. I don't want you to talk anymore. Don't speak. Feel. You just relax and enjoy."

Like she could relax right now with every cell in her body screaming for him to get closer. "Nathan?"

Without warning, he dropped his hands and sat back. His eyebrows rose. "What?"

She didn't have an answer, so she said nothing. She'd rather wait and see how the whole thing would play out.

She let out a deep breath. "This is nuts."

"No. You asking me questions like the one you asked a few minutes ago is nuts. This is probably the only sane thing I've done in a long time. This is a two-way street. I'm willing to help you, but you've got to do something for me too."

"So this is your fantasy? Doing it sitting up on a couch? I have to say, I'm a little disappointed."

The smile dropped from her face when she got a good look at his eyes. For the first time in a long time, she realized she was in deep trouble.

His low chuckle reverberated around her. "This isn't my fantasy. Not even close."

"Then what is it?"

He didn't answer, but the look in his eyes told her all she needed to know. She was in so much trouble now.

Finally. It was about damned time, too.

THREE

Joy squirmed against the hard seat of the chair. Nathan's fantasy was one she hadn't expected. One she hadn't even realized would be a turn-on, but she'd never been so wet in her life.

Once he'd stripped her of the rest of her clothes, he'd brought in a chair from the kitchen and told her to sit. She hadn't been prepared for what he'd done after that. Even now, she was still shocked at the way she'd let him bind her ankles to the chair legs and tie her arms behind her back. She was naked, completely open and bared to him, and though the black silk scarf he'd tied around her eyes prevented her from seeing him, she could feel his heated gaze raking every inch of her body.

"Nathan?" She squirmed again, trying to get some relief from the incredible tension thrumming through her body. Going without sex for months had been a mistake. How could he possibly expect her to sit there like this when she was about to come out of her skin?

"Don't speak. Don't move."

He wanted her to hold still? She snorted. That wasn't even possible. "I can't help it. I'm going crazy here."

"We had this discussion already, Joy." This time he whispered in her ear. His hot breath fanned her cheek and she shivered. "You need to be quiet or I'll leave you like this until you are."

He brought his hands to her breasts, but instead of cupping them this time, he pinched her nipples between his thumbs and forefingers. The rough touch sent a spark of heat through her core, settling into a rush of moisture in her pussy.

Something inside warned her that he meant it, and she needed to learn, if only for tonight, to keep her big mouth shut. Her mouth had gotten her into trouble more times than she could count, but she wasn't about to let one of those times be tonight. She wasn't about to pass up what might be a once-in-a-lifetime opportunity.

"You asked me what my fantasy is," he continued, his tone pure sin. Gone was the easy-going, laid-back neighbor she'd known for months. In his place was a strong, self-assured man who made her whole body throb for release. "Right now, right here with you, this is what I want. Can you give me that?"

She debated asking him to untie her for all of two seconds, but in the end her body won out over her mind.

"Yes." For one night. After that, she'd have to take matters into her own hands.

Nathan watched Joy for her reaction, and he was a little bit surprised when she didn't fight him. Instead she nodded, and his cock went rock-hard. Part of him had been trying to chase her away, to make her see that she was nuts asking him to tell her anything, let alone his wildest fantasies.

The woman had no clue what she'd started. None. This wasn't his *wildest* fantasy. Far from it. But it was tame enough that he could share it with her without revealing too much about himself. There were things innocent little Joy wouldn't want to know.

Then again, maybe she wasn't as innocent as he'd first thought.

He glanced her over, taking in the flushed pink color of her skin, the way her nipples were pebbled, her parted lips and the way her tongue swiped across them from time to time.

And her pussy. Her lower lips glistened with her juices and he licked his lips. For two months, since he'd moved in across the hall, he'd been dying to get a taste of her. Tonight, he would finally get his chance. She'd all but dumped herself into his lap tonight, and though he'd spent the better part of the past few weeks trying to ignore what he already knew, he couldn't do it anymore. Her little stunt had taken the choice out of his hands. With her so close, so open and naked, he intended to take full advantage.

Without a word to her, he left the room and went into his bedroom, rummaging through the bottom drawer of his dresser until he found what he was looking for. *Perfect.* She wanted a fantasy, and he'd give her one. By the time he finished with her, she wouldn't even be able to walk.

It felt like an eternity had passed while Nathan left her sitting there, and in another five seconds Joy was going to tell him to take his fantasies and shove them. She could write the article without him and this waiting crap. It was one thing to tie her up and blindfold her. It was something she hadn't tried before, but she could get into it. Leaving her all alone was something totally different. It had been his idea that they act out his fantasies rather than her just writing down what he said, so why was he doing this?

In the next instant, she got her answer as a faint buzzing sound filled the room, along with Nathan's heavy, booted footsteps.

"Nathan?" She swallowed hard and licked her lips. "What are you doing?"

He didn't answer. Instead the buzzing grew louder and she heard his footsteps as he walked across the room toward her. She knew that buzzing sound. Heard a similar one every time she switched on one of her vibrators. What did he have planned? The possibilities made her mouth water.

His hand came down on her shoulder and she shifted on the chair. "Hold still, Joy. I want to make this good for you, but I can't if you won't listen to me."

A scathing reply waited on the tip of her tongue, but she held it back. She could lay into him for his domineering attitude later. Right now she was having too much fun to protest. To think, a few months ago she'd looked at all men as boring. Nathan had quickly made her see how wrong she'd been in that assumption.

The vibrator brushed across the curve of her breast and she shivered. A second later, it brushed her nipple. She arched her back into the touch, the sensations made a hundred times stronger since she couldn't see what he was doing. Couldn't move more than a few inches in any direction. She tugged at the ties holding her arms behind her back, but they wouldn't budge.

Nathan's deep chuckle filled her senses. He dragged the vibrator from one breast to the other and back again, teasing her nipples until he was driving her wild. She'd never been so hot for a man before. Any man. And in her life there had been more than a few. None of them were able to do for her in weeks what Nathan had managed in less than an hour. Why had she thought sleeping with him would be a bad idea?

If there had ever been a valid reason, she couldn't remember what it was now.

The vibrator left her skin, but the buzzing didn't stop. Soon she felt Nathan's palms on her thighs, spreading her legs even more. She let out a soft moan.

"When a woman is blindfolded," he whispered into her ear, "all her other senses are heightened."

Didn't she know it. Every touch seemed to sear her skin. His scent, crisp and masculine, filled the air around her. She heard his every movement, every breath and it made her feel in tune with him in a way that was foreign to her. It should have made her nervous, but instead it only made her hotter. The buzzing sound stopped, throwing the room into silence, and she sat up a little straighter. What did he have planned now?

The vibrator touched her lips and she flinched out of surprise.

"Suck it, Joy. Get it nice and wet for your pussy."

Her pussy didn't need any added lubrication, but when she opened her mouth to tell him that, he slipped the toy between her lips.

"That is so fucking hot. Do you know how beautiful you look to me right now?"

His murmured words spurred her on. She bobbed her head up and down the length of the vibrator, swirling her tongue over the head with each upstroke, hoping she was teasing him as much as he was teasing her. His soft groan let her know she was, and the thought made her smile.

Soon Nathan pulled the toy from her lips and the buzzing sound filled the room again. Her whole body tensed, her pussy softening in anticipation. He trailed the vibrator down her stomach, stopping to tease her skin at various points, before he brought it between her legs to stroke across her clit.

She clenched her hands into fists, her lips parting on a moan. Her breathing was heavy, jagged, and her throat had gone bone dry. Her nipples ached and the muscles of her pussy quivered. Three strokes of that toy across her clit were all it took for her body to explode into orgasm.

She rocked back and forth, her body only able to move a few inches. It was frustrating and stimulating at the same time—like nothing she'd ever felt before. Everything dissolved into light and sensation and she could barely catch her breath. Still he continued to tease her sensitive flesh, alternating between hard and soft touches, drawing the toy away only to press it back against her again.

The chair rocked with her movements as he took her further and further from her comfort zone, making her cry out and scream his name—and he had yet to actually touch her.

After what felt like an eternity, her breathing started to return to normal and she slumped against the bonds, waiting for Nathan to release her.

He didn't.

Instead, he brought the vibrator lower, trailing it over her sensitized folds until he reached the entrance to her cunt. He pushed it inside, sending another round of tremors through her body.

"Oh, my God." Her muscles gripped the smooth surface of the

vibrator and she bucked her hips against it. Nathan found her clit and he pinched it lightly between his thumb and forefinger. Sensation zinged from the spot out to her limbs, making her body tingle from head to toe. It seemed like she hung in limbo for an eternity, her movements uncontrolled and her eyes closed. The only thing she could focus on was Nathan and how he was making her feel.

By the time she came back to earth, her wrists and ankles had gone numb from straining against the bonds.

Nathan pulled the toy out of her and soon after, the buzzing stopped. She thought he would move away but he didn't. Instead she felt his tongue trail a hot, wet line up the inside of her thigh.

"Nathan, stop."

He stilled but nipped the tender skin of her outer lip. "You want this."

"I can't take any more. Twice is enough."

His laughter rumbled against her. "You can handle more."

His tongue dipped between her legs and swirled over her clit. It was the most amazing thing she'd felt in a long time and she canted her hips forward as much as she could, eager for more. The orgasm started over, building and building until her body burst into sensation. Her mind shut down and she could do nothing except rock against him, alternately screaming his name and begging him not to stop. The tremors seemed to go on forever and when he finally pulled his mouth away, her head dropped back, limp.

Nathan untied her and helped her stand, and he took off the blindfold.

She shivered at the look in his eyes. "That was your fantasy?" she asked, her voice barely above a whisper. Every now and then a delicious errant tremor raced through her.

He just shook his head and let out a sensual laugh.

"What's so funny?"

He leaned in and brushed a kiss across the side of her neck. "Yeah, that was one of my biggest fantasies—at least where you're involved."

"You've had fantasies about me before?"

He raised his eyebrows before nodding his head. "Every day. Does that surprise you?"

"Actually, yes." And it thrilled her too. He'd been thinking about her. It sent a little shiver straight to her toes.

She'd been thinking about him too. Too much. She'd never admit it to him though.

"You know what another of my biggest fantasies about you is?" Nathan asked.

Somehow, she didn't think they were talking about the article anymore. Surprisingly, she was okay with that.

He smiled at her and she shook right down to her toes.

Maybe a little more than okay.

"What?"

"I'll have to show you sometime. It's pretty simple, actually." The way his smile grew told her it was anything but.

FOUR

Nathan's cock felt ready to burst. If he didn't get inside Joy—now—he had a feeling he might explode. She was spent, probably wouldn't be able to stand for long, let alone hold herself up for what he had in mind. Instead, he took her hand and led her out the sliding door onto the small balcony. The cool night air brushed his skin but did nothing to ease the heat coursing through him. The woman was incredible. Why hadn't he seen it before?

He shook his head. He *had* seen it. That was why he'd avoided her for so long. He should still be avoiding her, rather than walking right into something he swore he never even wanted. He should, but he couldn't. With Joy this close, the lure was too strong to resist. He needed to keep her off balance by keeping her guessing, allowing him to stay in control for a little longer. If he let her see how she affected him yet, she'd run away before he got the chance to explain things. She wouldn't understand.

Panic raced across her gaze for a second, and he couldn't help leaning in to press a hard, fast kiss on her lips. She really was beautiful. Not in a conventional way, but in every way that mattered. He responded to her in ways he'd tried to deny for too long. As much as it aggravated him, it was well past time to stop denying.

In all honesty, *where* he had her didn't even matter anymore, just that it happened. But she wanted fantasies and he didn't mind giving them to her. Especially if it would keep her from learning the truth for a little bit longer. *That* confession was one he didn't want to make until it was absolutely necessary.

He stepped back and leaned against the wooden railing that overlooked the courtyard two stories below. "Are you okay with this?"

She cocked her head to the side, her eyes still glazed with remnants of lust. "Let me get this straight. The first fantasy was about tying a woman to a chair and making her come while you're still dressed?"

"No. That was a personal fantasy, not something that every man wants. I've wanted to have you helpless for a long time."

Her eyes darkened, but a shiver ran through her. Her nipples peaked again and he barely resisted the urge to put his mouth on them. That would come in time. Now there were more important things he needed to do. She was his. He'd known it the second he'd seen her, but he'd refused to admit it. Now he couldn't deny it and he needed to show her where she belonged.

"Aren't you worried about someone seeing us?" she asked, her tone uncertain. "This is a pretty big apartment complex."

"It's two in the morning. I don't think that'll be a problem."

She didn't protest further. Instead she walked over to him, cupped his face in her hand and kissed him long and deep. She brought her other hand between them to caress his cock through the material of his jeans. Soon the first hand joined the second and, before he could protest, she'd unzipped his pants and freed his cock, circling the hard length of him in the heat of her palm.

Nathan broke the kiss and sucked in a breath. "If you keep touching me like that, I'm not going to last."

As it was, he'd been on edge since he'd tied her to the chair. He'd been fighting the urge to give up the whole fantasy angle, to bend her forward over the chair and ram into her for too long. Now she was touching him and his control was making a hasty retreat.

"You don't want to come?" The smile on her face told him she had revenge on her mind and he swallowed hard. "I'm very well sated, Nathan. I'm really not worried about how long you'll last."

"I thought this was supposed to be about my fantasies?"

She dropped to her knees in front of him. "It is."

In the next second, she'd slid her mouth over his cock and was bobbing her head up and down along the length. He let out a hard groan and tightened his hold on the railing behind him. She was an expert, and if she kept going he'd come before he even got inside her. That was the last thing he wanted.

She cupped his balls in one hand, giving them a gentle squeeze, while she continued to work his cock. Lost in the feel of her all around him, he closed his eyes and let his head drop back until she groaned against him. He looked down, shocked to find she'd slipped a hand between her legs. This turned her on as much as it did him. He smiled at the thought.

As much as he wanted her to continue, though, he couldn't let that happen tonight. Though she had an incredible mouth, he'd much rather come in her pussy. He nudged her head away, helped her stand and bent her over one of the wicker chairs on the deck. Her hands hit the surface, her ass coming up in the air. His smile widened. He'd give anything to sink his teeth into the skin of that full, rounded ass. *Anything.* So he did.

He leaned down and nipped at the tender skin just above her hip. She rewarded him with a harsh groan, her body pitching forward. "What are you doing?"

"Sorry. I couldn't help myself. You taste so good."

She laughed, but the sound was strained.

"You don't like biting?" he asked, only half teasing.

"Just the opposite. I like it too much."

Something told him they'd get along just fine.

His cock ached, more than ready to be satisfied, and he couldn't hold back any longer. He pressed it against her wet cunt, holding himself still for a few seconds before pushing inside. He didn't stop until he was fully seated. Joy was a tight fit and it thrilled him to think she could take all of him. Her muscles clamped down on him and he shuddered.

She squirmed back against him, prodding him to move. Though he tried to keep his strokes slow and measured, that didn't last long. Soon he couldn't do anything more than hold her hips in place while he pounded into her, relishing every hard stroke. Joy deserved gentle, easy loving after what he'd done earlier, but she wasn't going to get it tonight. Now that he was inside her, his mind started to shut down. He needed her so badly. Had for so long. He couldn't even think straight. The only thing he knew now was her scent and the feel of her hugging him so tight.

Mine.

The thought came out of nowhere, surprising him, but he didn't deny it. Couldn't. It was a fact that had slapped him in the face the second he'd gotten a whiff of that luscious, feminine scent.

He reached around and fingered her clit, knowing from her

soft exhales and the tremors racing through her that she was close. He owed it to her not to leave her hanging. Once he found his own release, it would be a while before he had the strength to go at it again.

The woman wanted a fantasy? He nearly laughed. She had no idea what she'd gotten herself into with him. Some of his fantasies might very well be her worst nightmares.

He wouldn't think about that now though. She didn't need to know anything more about him just yet.

His balls drew up tight against his body. If he counted to ten, over and over, maybe he could last. Just when he thought he couldn't take another second, Joy cried out his name and her inner muscles convulsed around him. The feel of her orgasm gave him the final push over the edge. The fingers of his free hand tight on her hip, he stroked hard into her as his release washed over him, threatening to tear him apart with its intensity. It was ages before he could think again, let alone move.

If he hadn't been sure about what she meant to him before, he was now, and that scared him more than anything.

FIVE

J oy zipped up her skirt. She had made plans to go out for a
quick bite with a few friends and was just about ready to go
when someone knocked on her apartment door. She glanced
in the peephole and saw Nathan standing in the hall.

"Shit," she muttered. For the past few days, since she'd run out
on him in the middle of the night, she'd been trying to think of
a way to explain to him what had happened. How could she explain it when she didn't even understand it herself? She unlocked
the door and pulled it open a crack. Just the sight of him, standing
there in worn jeans and a T-shirt, his feet bare, made her mouth
water. Her nipples pebbled, and there was no way she could hide
her reaction. All he'd have to do was look down at her thin, tight
shirt and he'd know. "Hi."

"Hi yourself."

His smile did funny things to her insides. Things she tried
to ignore. Ever since she'd left him sleeping in his bed after the
night they'd shared, she'd been trying to put what had happened
aside, knowing it would be best for both of them. So far, it wasn't

working. Seeing him only made her body—and her heart—ache. "What's going on?"

"I wanted to talk to you for a little while."

Not a good idea. *So* not a good idea. "I'm actually leaving right now. Meeting friends downtown. Can we talk tomorrow?"

"Come on, Joy. It'll only take a second."

She sighed and stepped back to let him in. Might as well get it over with. He was probably going to tell her he never wanted to see her again, that what had happened between them had been a mistake brought on by her unusual questions. They'd gotten carried away. The thought should have eased her mind, but for some reason it didn't.

"What's up?" She tried to plaster a bright smile on her face. No sense getting worked up over a one-night stand. And that's all they'd really had, despite her mind's insistence that something more had gone on between them.

The second she had the door closed, he pressed her up against it and kissed her.

She parted her lips in surprise and he delved his tongue inside, thrusting deep. His hands gripped her hips, pulling her tight against him as he continued his exploration of the recesses of her mouth. She held on tight, her head spinning and her world tilting on its axis. So maybe he hadn't come to tell her he didn't want to see her again. A giggle welled up inside her, quickly followed by a burst of heat. Damn, the man felt so good. It had only been two days, but somehow it felt like an eternity. Everything inside her ached for him. Maybe always had.

When he broke the kiss, she could barely remember her name. After clearing her throat and taking a few deep breaths, she was finally able to speak again. "I thought you said you wanted to talk?"

"I lied."

"So there isn't something you need to talk to me about?"

"No. Not now. Later." He didn't give her a chance to respond before he hiked her skirt up to her waist and lifted one of her legs around his hips. He ground his cock against her. His lips dipped down to the spot where her neck met her collar. His movements were fast, erratic, and her pussy got wet at the roughness of his touch. He wasn't smooth, but she liked him that way.

"Nathan?"

He glanced up at her long enough to shake his head. "Later." His hands tugged at her panties, pulling at them until the material tore away from her skin. A second later, the scrap of fabric dropped to the floor. His intensity should have made her nervous, but for some reason it only increased her arousal. She tugged at his shirt, eager to get it off his body.

He didn't give her a chance to look him over. Soon he lifted her other leg around his hip and he was inside her, stroking into her with a ferocity that slammed her back against the door. Half out of her mind with lust, she leaned forward and kissed the side of his neck. His moan encouraged her and he pulled her down against him, thrusting harder inside her. The orgasm that followed took her by surprise, stealing her breath.

Her lips tight on his neck, she bit down as her orgasm spiraled through her, dimly aware of the fact that Nathan's teeth had sunk into her shoulder. The sharp pain made her gasp. Her fingers dug into his shoulders and she held on tight, riding the waves along with him as his own release washed over him.

When he set her down on her feet, her whole body felt liquid.

"What time are you supposed to meet your friends?" he asked, his breathing as heavy as hers.

Was he kidding? No way was she walking away from him now.

"I'm not going. Suddenly I'm not feeling very hungry any-more." At least not for food. "Can you stay tonight?"

The smile on his face told her he would.

W hy did you walk out the other night?" Nathan stroked the flat of his palm down Joy's side, loving the little shiver that ran through her when he got to her hip. She was ticklish, and it made him smile.

She rolled to her side and kissed him—a long, leisurely kiss full of affection but not lust. After he'd nearly attacked her against her front door, they'd moved to the bed and spent a good few hours getting to know each other a lot better. No clothes, no fantasies between them. Just the two of them. It was a scene that normally would have made him uncomfortable, but with her, it felt almost . . . right.

"I don't know why I left. It was too intense, I guess. I wasn't looking for anything permanent."

"Have you changed your mind now?"

A small smile graced her full lips. "Maybe. I guess we'll just have to wait and see."

"You scare me. Do you know that?"

She blinked. "Why would I scare you?"

"It's hard to explain. This just feels so right. It shouldn't so soon."

"Then I guess we'll have to spend some time exploring the possibilities." Her lips parted on a yawn. "But not now. I need to catch a few hours first."

He leaned in to her neck and drew a deep breath of her rich, heady scent. It would be forever imprinted on his mind after to-night. Somehow the thought didn't make him nearly as nervous as he thought it should.

Nathan wandered into the kitchen, parched and in need of a drink. It was an odd feeling, being so thirsty that he was afraid a simple glass of water wouldn't do. After the workout she'd put him through though, it made sense. He hadn't even had a chance to have dinner before he'd gone to see her the night before, and they certainly hadn't taken a break for something as time-consuming as a meal.

He yawned and stretched, his mind flashing back to the night with Joy. It had been amazing. No pretenses, no articles or questions to get in the way. Just the two of them and hot, freakin' incredible sex. And talking. He'd never been one for much talking before, but he found he wanted to get to know her better on more than just the carnal level. He could really get used to her being around. The thought would have scared him once, but now it only made him think of the possibilities.

He opened the fridge, his eyes still bleary, but the only things he found inside turned his stomach. Blood bags. Lots of them. *What the fuck?*

He stood up and slammed the fridge closed, his fingers going to his neck and the spot she'd bitten the night before. Two tiny raised lumps alerted him to what he probably should have suspected a lot sooner. Would have suspected, had he not been so wrapped up in denying that he wanted her.

How in the hell had this happened?

"Nathan?"

He spun to find Joy standing in the doorway, wrapped in the sheet they'd torn off the bed.

"Why do you have a fridge full of blood?" And why the fuck had he *not known*?

"I can explain."

His knees buckled and he had to lean back against the counter. Somehow he doubted he'd like her explanation.

Given the recent discovery, she'd like his confession even less.

SIX

Joy stood in the door, blocking Nathan's only escape from the kitchen. She couldn't let him leave now. Not until she'd had a chance to explain. If he ran out of here now, all kinds of trouble would happen.

"You're a vampire."

It wasn't a question but a statement instead. She nodded, frowning at the fact that he didn't look at her like she was nuts. He looked shocked but not altogether surprised.

"For real?" He gave a little nervous laugh that seemed to be out of character. "No way. This can't be happening. I don't do vampires."

Not really the reaction she'd been expecting. Or the one she'd been hoping for. Since their first night together she'd envisioned the moment he'd find out over and over in her head, playing out all the possible scenarios. This one hadn't even made the list. "What are you talking about?"

"Exactly what I said. I don't *do* vampires."

"Excuse me?"

He pushed away from the counter and paced the length of the kitchen, running his hand through his dark hair. His jeans rode low on his hips, revealing a tantalizing amount of skin below. Suddenly he stopped and faced her, his eyes narrowed. "You bit me."

"Sorry. I'd planned on going out to feed last night, but you sort of got in the way."

"You probably shouldn't have done that."

"I said I was sorry. I didn't take much. Just enough to get me through the night. You bit me too. Pretty hard, I might add."

"And that's exactly what the problem is. If I'd known about your little issue, I never would have done that."

He made it sound like she'd deliberately kept something from him. Well, she had, but not because she didn't want him to know. Because she'd been afraid of his reaction. Most humans would have laughed and told her to find psychiatric help. "What are you talking about?"

"I'm a werewolf."

Her stomach bottomed out and she had to lean against the door frame for support. *Oh shit.* This couldn't be happening. "You're a what?" Her voice came out as nothing more than a squeak.

"A werewolf. You know, all furry and howling at the moon?" He took a few steps closer but then seemed to change his mind and backed up again. "Do you know it only takes a bite from a werewolf to become one? Just one bite. It's the saliva that does it. All it takes is a little bit."

She whimpered. Her breath caught in her lungs and she had to pound her fist on her chest to get it back. "Why did you bite me so hard?"

"I didn't mean to, damn it. You bit me first, and instinct kicked in and I sort of went out of my mind."

"You couldn't control yourself?" Something in the way he said those words thrilled her. She made him lose control. How long had she waited to hear that from a man?

Okay, so it was very possible that the man had turned her into a werewolf, but the idea still made a smile tickle the corners of her mouth. How much worse could it really be? She was already a vampire. Would going furry every once in a while be that much of a big deal?

No. But at the same time, she knew it would. She sighed. Why had she ever wished to get rid of the boredom? She certainly wasn't bored anymore. And she had a pretty good suspicion it would be a while before she could claim she was bored again.

"No. I couldn't. That's actually what I came here to talk to you about last night, before things got out of hand." He took a deep breath as if steeling himself for his explanation. "I wanted you the second I saw you. No, it was more than that. I've always been told that I'll know my mate when I see her, but I never believed it until I saw you."

So that was what he thought she was? His mate? She blinked back in surprise. She wasn't even his kind.

"Don't tell me you don't feel it too," he continued, walking closer until he was only inches away. He cupped her face in his palm. "I know you feel something for me that's more than lust. I see it in your eyes whenever you look at me."

Was he stupid? Of course she did. Had for a long time, but she hadn't been willing to admit it. She hadn't even known him properly until a few days ago, and admitting that she wanted him in her life had seemed crazy right up until this moment. It still seemed crazy, but a little less so in light of recent events. "Okay, for the sake of argument, say I do feel a little something. What's going to happen now, anyway?"

"You've been bitten, Joy. I would imagine, since you're techni-cally human, all your reactions will be the same. You'll be able to change."

She wrinkled her nose. He said it like it was some kind of priv-ilege, when she had a feeling it would be a long time before she thought of it as anything more than creepy. "Like at the full moon?"

He laughed, though the expression on his face was still seri-ous. "No. Whenever you want to. Once you've made the change a few times, it'll come easily to you."

"What about you?"

The look he gave her was full of confusion.

"In order for a human to become a vampire, an exchange of blood has to occur. Even a small exchange will do it. You bit me, I bit you. Are you getting the picture yet?"

His eyes widened and he dropped his hand. "Shit."

"My thoughts exactly."

"So where do we go from here?"

She shrugged. "I have no clue. I guess we'll just have to wait and see."

A smile broke out over his face and she couldn't help but smile back. All these weeks of pining after her neighbor, and she'd never imagined it would work out like this. It wasn't what she'd wanted, but now that she had it she couldn't say she was disappointed. All in all, it would prove to be a very interesting life.

EPILOGUE

Nathan watched Joy step out of the darkness and walk toward him. His heart skipped a beat. Two years. It had been two years since fate—and a few little accidents—had brought them together. Now that he had her, he intended to never let her go. There were dozens of women at his brother's engagement party, yet he'd barely noticed any of them.

She reached him and wrapped her arms around his neck, planting a long, wet kiss on his lips before she stepped back and laughed. Her gaze drifted to his brother Tyler and his bride-to-be. "Cute couple."

"Yeah." He put his arm around Joy's shoulder and pulled her closer. "Why didn't we ever have anything like this?"

She rolled her eyes. "Because we're not getting married, silly."

"Want to?"

Her gaze flew to his, her lips parted. It took her a few seconds to answer. "Are you serious?"

"Yep." He'd been thinking about it for a while. A good six months at least. Maybe even longer. She meant everything to him, and he honestly didn't know what had taken him so long to ask. It had just slipped out, but now that he'd said the words he realized he'd been waiting to say them for a long time.

Joy said nothing for so long he thought she might turn him down. But finally, *finally*, she smiled. "That's got to be the most unconventional proposal I've ever heard."

"Is that a yes?"

"Uh-huh. But you have to do something for me first."

"What's that?"

"You have to tell your family."

That was all she wanted? That was an easy request. "My family loves you. In fact, my mom's been bugging me for way too long to pop the question."

"That's not what I'm talking about." She glanced up at him, the look in her eyes nothing short of wicked. "You need to tell them that you're a vampire now, too."

He sighed. Yeah, he did need to spill that little secret. He'd planned on keeping it to himself for as long as he could, but if that was what Joy wanted, he'd give it to her. "Okay. But let me do it my own way."

"Thanks, Nathan. I love you, you know."

He leaned down and kissed the top of her head, already planning what he'd say to his mother. No matter what happened, it would end up being an interesting conversation. "I love you, too."

VIRGIN
SEEKS
BAD-ASS BOY

Ruth D. Kerce

ONE

lice Sutherland spotted Caleb Sawyer crouched down, working on his motorcycle in the driveway, like he did most Saturday afternoons. Fascinated, she stood on her porch, watching him from across the street.

He'd moved into the neighborhood a little over a year ago, and he'd caught her eye immediately. Hell, more than that. She practically drooled whenever she saw him. Tall, built, confident— a woman's dream.

She wasn't the only one taken by his assets either. More than one beautiful woman had spent the night with him since he'd moved in. Not that she made a habit of spying, but she couldn't help noticing when a woman came from his house early in the morning, particularly if she was out watering her shrubs.

He glanced up briefly, and her heart thudded. No. She hadn't caught his attention. Just a barking dog from down the street. She thought for a moment that maybe he'd felt her watching him.

The truth about the man was undeniable. Caleb Sawyer exuded sex—wild, rough, nasty sex. Enough to fulfill any woman's darkest desires. And that assessment wasn't just in her fantasies.

One day, she'd taken a short cut through an alley, just off their street, on her way back from a nearby park. Normally, the alley was empty, but that day she saw Caleb there with his motorcycle, and a woman.

He had her pinned over the bike, her skirt flipped up over her butt, and was fucking her hard from behind. One hand tangled in her hair while the other curled around her hip, and he kept asking her if she liked it rough.

Alice wasn't sure what the woman had said. She'd been too turned on by the sight of Caleb and his actions to care about anything else. His leather jacket had covered his upper torso, but his jeans hung low, and his tight, firm ass had been bared to her view. So sexy!

When he'd stopped fucking and started spanking the woman, Alice had almost moaned aloud, picturing herself pinned over the motorcycle, his hand slapping *her* ass instead. When he continued fucking the blonde, she imagined him thrusting his cock into her own pussy until she screamed and came, preferably more than once.

Not wanting to completely invade his privacy—though she would have loved to see him come—she'd turned around and gone the other way, barely able to walk, her legs trembled so badly. She hadn't been able to get that image of Caleb out of her mind since.

That's when she knew for certain that she wanted him. No man had ever affected her so strongly or made her pussy throb so hard. Caleb was just the type of man she'd been searching for . . . for her first time.

No more waiting.

After that day, she'd tried to attract his attention whenever they met at the mailbox or during block parties. He was always nice to her, and they even shared an interest in classic films, but he didn't seem to catch on to the sexual hints she kept sending him. She'd finally decided to be more direct.

Even though it was cool out today, he wore only a deep blue, short-sleeved T-shirt tucked into well-worn jeans. His black boots gleamed as if he'd just polished them. The way his muscles bunched and relaxed as he moved, like some predator, made her tingle all over. She'd had many a fantasy of running her fingers through his thick brown hair, over his bare chest and down to his cock. Oh, yes.

If she was going to do this, she needed to do it now, while the opportunity existed. "Time to turn fantasy into reality," she murmured.

Taking a deep breath, she walked down the two concrete steps, along the path, over the sidewalk, paused, then crossed the street and continued up his drive. So far, so good. She gathered all her strength and forced her voice to work, hoping she sounded less nervous than she actually felt.

"Hi, Caleb."

He glanced up, then returned to fiddling with the bike. "Hey, Ali. You're home early from the library today."

She loved the way he called her Ali. No one else did, and she thought it sounded sexy. "I'm not working this weekend."

Continuing with his repairs, he grunted in response.

She knew on weekends he didn't go into the motorcycle shop he partially owned. So, she'd coordinated her schedule with his to have the time available to put her plan into motion. "Can I tell you something?"

He glanced up but only for a moment. "What?"

Her heart pounded against her ribs. *Here we go.* "I'm . . . I'm still a virgin."

At twenty-four years old, she was sick of waiting for "Mr. Right" and was determined to sleep with a man who could make her toes curl and all her sexual fantasies come true. Caleb was that man.

He stopped working. He didn't look at her, but she saw his hand tighten on the wrench he held. After a moment, he continued tightening whatever he was tightening. "And?"

"And?" she repeated in confusion. That wasn't quite the response she'd expected.

"I'm assuming after a statement like that, there's an 'and' attached."

The man was too smart for his own good. "Well, yes." Her stomach fluttered, and she felt a little lightheaded at the thought of his large hands stroking her breasts, her pussy, the soft skin between her thighs, her ass. She could hardly wait.

"I want you to de-virgin me."

No response. He simply continued working. Hmm. Okay, this didn't bode well.

"Did you hear me?"

"I heard."

"Well?" She felt a bead of perspiration slide between her breasts.

"Forget it, Ali."

What? Forget it? Just like that? His quick answer and casual attitude not only surprised but irked her. Weren't men always on automatic or something when it came to sex? He could at least have the decency to look up and appear shocked.

Because of the different women she saw over here, she'd been so certain . . . No. She shook her head. She refused to get upset or rattled in front of him. He wasn't worth it. Not on an emotional level. She didn't even know him really. His body was the only thing she wanted. Well, maybe not only his body, but that's as much as she'd allowed herself to expect or hope for from him.

Okay, fine. He had turned her down. If the sex alone wasn't enough of a temptation, she was prepared to offer him an additional incentive. She raised her chin and made sure her voice came out sounding strong and confident. "I'll pay you."

The wrench fell from his hand, and he surged to his feet. "Excuse me?" He towered over her.

His green eyes practically burned her skin with their intensity. She backed up a step and clutched her hands together but didn't run, not about to let him intimidate her into changing her mind. "I'll pay you for one weekend of your time."

"You want to pay me to fuck—"

"Stop!" She put her hands up as if to ward off his words. As soon as the protest left her mouth, she regretted it. *Great.* Now she sounded like a prude as well as a virgin. She wasn't a prude. He'd just caught her off guard.

"Believe me, princess, you don't want a guy like me pumping away at your pussy, especially your first time. Go find yourself a nice, safe, respectable librarian."

He'd put that crudely on purpose. "I'm not a princess, and I don't want someone safe. I want wild and passionate!"

"Wild and passionate, huh?" He hesitated and then a gleam entered his eyes. "All right, lower your pants, lean over the bike and I'll fuck you right here. We'll put on a show for the neighbors." His hand brushed across his crotch.

Her gaze lowered a moment, following the movement, then snapped back to his eyes. "That's not funny."

"It wasn't meant to be. I'm into kink, baby. On the edge, hard, rough, down-and-dirty fucking."

She couldn't help but recall the image of him in the alley. Her pussy clenched in need. Wouldn't he be surprised if she said okay? On-the-edge sex was just what she wanted from him, after all. She almost laughed at the thought of saying so, just to see the look on his face. Instead, she shrugged. "Obviously, I want something private and tender too."

His eyes held almost a humorous look now, and one side of his mouth hitched into a half-smile. "You think I can give you all that—wild, passionate *and* tender?"

She nodded.

"Well, I'm flattered. But I'm not your guy."

"I want to have sex with you, Caleb."

His eyebrows shot up, as if not expecting her to push the issue once he refused.

Appearing from the opposite side of a line of bushes, two elderly ladies strolled by. Oh, goodness! They nodded at her and Caleb as they passed. She hoped the women hadn't heard anything. She didn't want the entire neighborhood to know her business.

Caleb curled his fingers around her arm. "Let's take this conversation inside." He dragged her through his garage and into the house, slamming the back door closed behind them. He released her arm and plowed his fingers through his hair. "You can't just go around asking men to . . . to have sex with you, Ali."

"I haven't been. Yet. Only you."

His lips thinned, and a muscle in his jaw ticced. He paced, grumbled something under his breath she didn't understand then stopped directly in front of her. But he remained in profile, staring at the wall, as if unwilling to look into her eyes.

He seemed totally uninterested in her proposal, darn it. So much for her plans. Now would be a good time to walk out on him, except he blocked her path to the back door.

His nostrils flared as he took in a deep breath then released it. Finally, he spoke. "Why come to me? I'm sure you work with plenty of men you could ask."

Not really, and she saw no reason to prolong this torture with a question and answer session. She supposed she'd have to resort to "Plan B" now. Despair filled her more than she'd expected. She really wanted Caleb.

"Forget it." She used his words. They were, after all, to the point. "Forget I said anything about sex at all." She turned to leave through the front.

His hand on her arm stopped her. "Wait. Look at me, Ali." His voice came out soft but firm. "Look at me," he repeated in a stronger tone when she didn't immediately meet his eyes.

Caleb's heart raced. His jeans felt uncomfortably tight. He'd grown hard the moment "de-virgin me" had spilled from Ali's lips—the last thing he'd expected from her. And the most erotic thing he'd heard in a long time, especially coming from such a full, pouty mouth.

Her confession more than surprised him. He couldn't remember ever seeing her with a steady guy but never gave it much thought. Though not classically beautiful, she possessed a gorgeous mouth meant for kissing and sucking a man's dick, sparkling green eyes that drew people in, and a suppressed sexiness that he wouldn't mind seeing unleashed. She hadn't run when he'd tried to scare her away either. Impressive.

This time she met his eyes full on. "What?"

"Why do you want to do this?" he asked, intrigued.

"Why do I want to have sex?"

He smiled indulgently. "Why do you want to have sex with me?" Somehow, the answer mattered to him, and more than he thought it should.

"I told you. Besides, you're really hot and have always been nice to me." She raised her chin a notch. "Until today. See, I thought you were probably good at sex. I notice women over here all the time."

All the time was a bit of an exaggeration, he thought, but he would like to think he was good at sex. A smile tugged at his lips. He'd never heard any complaints, nor had any problems getting a woman into bed. The fact that she thought him hot, and actually said so, was a huge turn-on to him. He couldn't imagine the courage it had taken her to approach him about taking her virginity.

He studied her a moment, suddenly wondering if she might be playing him for some reason. She was a little old to still be a virgin. No. The anxious look in her eyes told him that this situation was indeed very real for her.

"I know you wouldn't want anything more from me, Caleb. So things would stay uncomplicated."

He felt the frown that claimed his features. Why would she assume that? Did he come across as that cold and self-centered? Just *come* and go, so to speak? Okay, yeah. Maybe he had done that, and more than once. But her thinking that was just the way he acted with women bothered him.

"Also . . . " she started, but then let the sentence hang.

"Yeah?" He prompted when she hesitated to continue. She suddenly looked quite nervous. "What, Ali?"

"Well, truthfully, I want a man who can introduce me to some darker fantasies."

His cock responded to that. Oh, yes. "Like what?" he asked, his voice low and deep.

"Like, um, what I saw in the alley, with you and that blonde."

It took him a moment to figure out what she was talking about. Ah, right. The alley. "You saw that? You watched?" The idea set his heart pounding. He remembered that day, that encounter.

"Just for a minute."

The thought of her watching intrigued him. "You should have come up and joined us." A smile crossed his face. "That would have been a dark fantasy come true." He waited for her to be appalled or offended, but she just stood there, looking him straight in the eye. Damn, she was sexy as hell. Ready and willing to test out her body and apparently any type of sex he might want to involve her in. The erotic possibilities played through his mind until a disturbing thought struck him. "If I say no to you, do you have a second candidate in mind for your de-virgin . . . ing?"

A moment passed before she answered as if deciding whether to tell him or not. "Well, actually, yes. And you *did* say no."

She was right. He'd already told her to find another man. Still, his chest tightened at her answer. No telling what kind of jerk she'd picked out. Why he cared, he didn't know. But he did care. "Who?"

"Ed Morton from down the street."

"Ed Morton!" Caleb grabbed her arm. "He's married and twice your age, Ali!" No way was he letting Morton at her first.

She pulled out of his grasp. "He's divorced, and he's not that old. He just doesn't take care of himself."

"He's divorced? Since when?"

"Two months ago. He kinda came on to me at the mailbox the other day and told me everything had been finalized. He wants me to come over for dinner and videos next week. And just so you know, all the men I work with are married. So, you and Ed became my top choices. Though you've always been my number one."

Her last sentence came out as a whisper, and he saw the vulnerability in her eyes. Touched by her words about him, and mortified by her words about Ed, Caleb had a hard time thinking straight.

The disturbing image of Ed Morton came to mind. That jerk jumped any woman with air in her lungs. His wife must have finally caught on. He just imagined the type of videos Ed planned for their date, if he got Ali alone. Not film classics, for sure, unless classic porn counted. She deserved better than Ed. Of course, she deserved better than him too, but . . . "Don't ask him, Ali," he heard himself saying almost before he realized it.

"Oh?" A hopeful gleam entered her eyes. "Does that mean you'll do it?"

Caleb shook his head. A virgin. How had he gotten himself into this? What the hell was he thinking? Stupid question. He knew what he was thinking . . . and not your normal schoolboy fantasies. He might live to regret this, but the offer to fuck her was too good to pass up. "Okay, yeah, I'll do it." At least she'd be safe with him. Morton probably wouldn't even want to use a rubber.

"Today?"

She was an eager little thing. He liked that, and so did his dick, which twitched in anticipation. "Yes, today." He raised his hand to stroke her cheek then realized he was still dirty and smelly from working on the bike. He let his hand drop. "Will you stay while I put the bike away and get cleaned up?"

Although she'd mentioned an interest in the darker side of sex, she still might come to regret not choosing a tender-touch, soft-words kind of guy. But he'd warned her. Once he got through with Ali, she would be far from the virginal woman who stood before him now.

Alice's pulse raced, and her breath caught in her throat. He wanted her to stay. *Yes.*

She nodded, unable to voice her assent aloud. She'd probably stutter like an idiot. Her fantasy, and with her fantasy lover, was about to become a reality.

"I won't be long." Caleb turned and went back into the garage.

She stood there staring toward the door, not sure what to do with herself. "I can't believe this is actually happening," she whispered, then giggled as her nerves bubbled to the surface. Good nerves, of anticipation. A few minutes later she heard the garage door come down and the back door open.

"Make yourself comfortable," Caleb called out, then disappeared into what she assumed was his bedroom.

Feeling more than a little out of place, she gingerly sat on his brown leather couch and put her hands between her knees. Finally, sex.

She hoped not to be disappointed. Though she couldn't imagine that happening with Caleb. She knew women who hated sex and others who loved it. She wanted to be in the "love it" category. She masturbated but never penetrated herself. All her touching was clitoral, and she'd never had much of a climax. With Caleb, she hoped for a highly satisfying experience. Hell, she wanted more than highly satisfying. She wanted to shake and scream out from the pleasure.

She glanced toward the window. It would be dark soon. Would

he want to just get it over with or would he take her out on a date first? Her heart beat heavily in her chest. She didn't know if she could survive a date, knowing what would happen afterward.

Vaguely, she registered that his house appeared neat and a lot cleaner than she'd expected for a guy on his own. She liked that. A pleasant odor even drifted through the air—vanilla. She scooted back on the couch cushion. After a moment, she leaned her head back and closed her eyes, trying to relax as best she could.

Waiting was never her strong suit. Waiting for sex, well, talk about stress!

Another nervous giggle threatened, but she squashed it. She wondered how she'd feel about her decision to do this after the weekend was over . . .

TWO

"Ali?"

Her eyes fluttered open. It seemed as if only a moment had passed, but she noticed the first shadows of dusk through the window. She must have fallen asleep.

Caleb stood in front of her, his hair moist from a shower. Wrapped around his waist, he wore a deep green bath towel, the exact color of his eyes, and nothing more. Major hunk alert! His bare chest, so broad and strong, made her feel very feminine all of a sudden.

He held out his hand. "Are you ready?" He smiled slightly. "Or have you come to your senses and changed your mind?"

Tremors racked her body. She wasn't sure her legs would even support her. Sexual excitement rushed through her, making her skin tingle. "I haven't changed my mind, Caleb. I'm ready." No way was she passing up the opportunity to feel his body against hers, inside hers.

Apparently he just wanted to get on with it, which was fine with her. She liked that he had cared enough about her feelings to shower first. She slowly stood, taking his hand to steady herself.

His warm, strong fingers closed around hers, making her feel safe and secure. But when she met his gaze, the hungry look in his eyes made her feel anything but safe.

"You sure you don't want to take some time to rethink this and maybe wait for a guy who's ready to give you a commitment, Ali?"

He must have seen the nervousness in her gaze, felt the trembling in her hand, to give her yet another opportunity to run. "I'm sure. I've already spent too much time thinking and waiting." And that was the truth. Now that he'd agreed, she didn't intend to let Caleb get away from her.

"All right. Just remember, you asked for this."

The tone in his voice gave her a moment's pause and her step faltered. She wondered if his bedroom would be all leather, filled with whips and blindfolds and sex toys. He'd said he liked kink. He might have erotic art on the walls, a mirror on the ceiling, sex-enhancing drugs on hand. She swallowed hard. No telling what he was leading her into. She raised her chin, prepared to face whatever erotic experiences he had in mind for a definite night to remember.

He showed her into a dimly lit bedroom. A massive king-sized bed with a mirrored headboard took up most of the room. Black covers were neatly turned down to reveal beige sheets. Green candles flickered atop the dresser. Soft music wafted in the background, barely audible. Not some dark den of lust as she'd imagined. He'd made the room romantic for her. The thoughtful gesture tugged at her heart. "Oh, Caleb."

"Is the room okay?"

He was being so nice, so gentle, that she felt like crying. "It's perfect. Thank you."

"The first time should be special."

The smile that crossed his face warmed her trembling limbs. He'd gone through more preparation than she'd expected from him. Her motorcycle-riding bad boy possessed a tender heart, just as she'd always suspected.

"I—I don't know what I'm supposed to do." The words popped out, and she suddenly wished she could take them back. They made her sound naïve, which she really wasn't, just inexperienced. She knew that planning her deflowering—geez, she hated that term—would kill the spontaneity and probably a lot of the passion, but it had been the only way to get the man she wanted.

Caleb looked into her eyes. "Do you trust me?"

She let her gaze lock with his, and she realized that she truly did trust him to give her a great sexual experience. "Yes."

"You shouldn't," he whispered.

At his warning, her pulse raced. Had she gotten in over her head here for her first time? She was trusting a man she really didn't know to take her virginity. But at the same time, she'd never felt so turned on. Yes, Caleb was worth the risk.

He pushed a stray strand of hair behind her ear. His fingers brushed her neck, and his thumb eased across her bottom lip. "May I kiss you?"

That he had asked permission surprised her and just endeared him more in her heart. She nodded and wet her lips with the tip of her tongue, grazing along the same path his thumb had taken. When his eyes darkened, her heart pounded so hard it hurt. She wondered what he was feeling. Lust? Excitement? Deep longing? She certainly felt all those things.

Caleb leaned down and brushed his lips across hers. Gently. Barely connecting. Only their mouths touched, and when he pulled back, instead of deepening the kiss as she'd expected, she moaned her disappointment.

"I love your soft moans." His hand slid around the back of her neck, holding her in place. "Let's see how many of those I can coax out of you." He glanced down her body. Her pulse raced faster and perspiration gathered under her hairline. She felt as if he saw right through her clothing.

His fingers toyed with the top button of her blouse. "I love breasts like yours, Ali. A mouthful and more. I'm going to suck your nipples until you beg me to shove my cock into your pussy and fuck you hard."

Her breath caught. The image of his mouth on her breasts and his cock inside her, torturing her with exquisite delight, almost made her come right there. "Yes," she replied, barely above a whisper.

One button at a time popped open under his fingers. She was amazed at how expertly he worked as he held her steady, his other hand still behind her neck. If she hadn't looked down, she wouldn't even have felt him undressing her.

He released her neck and stepped behind her, slowly sliding the orchid-colored, long-sleeved blouse down her shoulders. His fingers skimmed her bare flesh, causing her to sigh. She was glad she'd worn her sexiest bra and panties. The pink lace against her pale skin and light-brown hair looked enticing, even to her. She hoped Caleb liked the garments.

His finger slid under one bra strap. "Pretty. Did you wear this for me?"

"Yes."

He turned her around and his fingers brushed across her lace-covered nipples.

"Oh." She felt his touch like a hot spark right through the

fabric. If that small brush of her breasts affected her like no man or fantasy she'd ever experienced, she didn't know how she'd withstand the intensity of his touch when he purposely tried to arouse her.

Caleb leaned in, and his warm breath tickled her neck. He didn't kiss her, just hovered close. His nearness, and soft nuzzling, had her completely under his spell. She moaned softly.

"So sexy, Ali. I'm going to lick you all over, baby."

She practically melted at his feet. He touched the front clasp of her bra, and in the next instant, her breasts spilled out. She saw his throat work as he swallowed hard.

"Ali." He dropped the lace garment to the floor, "you're beautiful. Such sexy breasts with rosy nipples that any man would kill to suck."

She felt a blush creep up her neck. Damn. She never blushed. His words made her crazy with physical need. "Touch me, Caleb," she whispered, her tone close to pleading.

"Yes, ma'am." He smiled. "My pleasure."

She expected his hands to cover her breasts first, him to maybe tweak her nipples with his fingers. Instead, he leaned down and swiped his tongue across one hard bud. *Oh, my!* She grasped his shoulders.

"Ah, you like that."

"Yes!" The texture and moistness of his tongue dragging across her ultra-sensitive nipple felt incredible and sent a thrill right down to her toes.

"Come here. I want to up the intensity level." He took her hand and led her over to the bed. He sat down and drew her into his lap, holding her close. He thumbed her moist nipple. "You're going to feel this all the way down to your cunt, baby."

He leaned her back and lowered his head to suck the nipple into his mouth.

Ali's fingers clung to his hair. "Oh, Caleb." She did feel his sucking all the way down to her pussy, as if he were stimulating her clit at the same time. He was so right. The words "Fuck me, Caleb!" perched right on the tip of her tongue, ready to spill out.

He sucked and licked until she trembled and felt on the edge of something more powerful than she'd ever experienced. Yes! After a particularly delightful swirl of his tongue, Caleb raised his head.

No, damn it! She'd been so close to what felt like a massive orgasm. "Don't stop!"

"I decide tonight. Not you." He laid her fully on the bed then stood up and dropped his towel.

A gasp escaped her before she could stop it. Completely naked now, the whole picture of his well-toned body struck her. Caleb was indeed a woman's dream. Strong, muscular but not overly muscle-bound. Perfect. The light dusting of dark hair that covered his chest narrowed to a thin line leading down to his cock, which held her undivided attention.

Long, hard, thick. She doubted she'd be able to get her fingers completely around the shaft. The ridges and slight curve of his cock fascinated her. The purplish-red head, much larger than she'd expected, made her body flush and flooded her with desire. She couldn't help but wonder what that tip tasted like. She reached out. "I want to touch you." That impressive cock soon would be inside her—thrusting, pumping, filling her up.

"Not yet. Open your pants for me, Ali. Now."

She gulped at his near order but complied. With shaky fingers, she reached down and undid her belt, popped the button on her pants and then slowly lowered the zipper.

"Watching a woman undress always gets me hot. Faster. Show me how eager you are for my cock."

When she fumbled, her fingers not cooperating very well, he stepped forward and pulled her pants and hose off, leaving only her pink lace panties. She gasped at the abrupt move. He probably thought she was about to change her mind. Little did he know.

"There's no turning back now, Ali."

At his in-charge manner and tone of his voice, her pussy flooded with moisture and she nodded. *Oh, how I want this!*

Her mouth dropped open when he turned to fold her clothing, her blouse and bra included, and placed them on the dresser, well away from the candles. Only when she saw the small smile on his face did she realize he'd done the folding on purpose to stall . . . to drive her crazy from the waiting and to extend the anticipation.

Finally, he returned to the bed, the look on his face all serious once more. She felt so decadent, lying on the mattress almost completely naked, with him staring down at her, his eyes filled with fire, raking her body one slow inch at a time.

Caleb stretched out beside her and glided his palm over her abdomen. His fingers eased under the top band of her panties.

She gulped.

But he went no farther. He stared into her eyes. "You're gorgeous. Why have you waited so long to have sex?"

Gorgeous. He sure knew how to make a woman feel good. Her clit throbbed. She needed his intimate touch. Her hips rose slightly of their own volition.

"Tell me." His fingers slid lower but not low enough to satisfy her need.

Looking deeply into his sexy, green eyes, she felt mesmerized.

"I never wanted to settle, simply to have someone in my life . . . in my bed."

"Well, I am impressed by your control. Tonight it ends. I'm going to make you need sex from now on, Ali. Crave it more than you ever thought possible." He kissed her lips, and his fingers massaged the skin just above the hairline of her pussy. When she opened her mouth, his tongue entered, exploring and tasting.

Oh, yes. Her nails grazed his chest, and she felt him shudder. She liked that she could affect him physically.

His fingers teased her, moving back and forth along her skin. Caleb slid down her body and placed soft kisses between her breasts. His tongue swiped one nipple then the other, making her arch beneath him. His hand slid down another couple of inches, and his fingers tangled in her pussy hair.

"Oh, Caleb, yes." He had the best tongue, the best touch.

He sucked a nipple into his mouth and drew hard.

Ali jerked. "Caleb! Oh!" Her hips moved, trying to force his fingers inside her pussy. When he nibbled on the hard bud in his mouth and then bit down gently, she almost lost it. "Please! I need more, Caleb. Please. Fuck me! Fuck me right now!"

He nibbled down her ribs to her stomach, causing waves of pleasure to roll through her. He licked at her navel, then lower.

Sensations exploded everywhere he touched her. If she'd known it would be this intense, she'd have approached him much sooner.

He slowly withdrew his fingers.

No! She grabbed at him.

He forced her hands to her breasts. "Play with your nipples. Pinch them."

She swallowed hard but did as he told her, sending a thrill down her body. Oh, this was so hot!

The fingers of both his hands curled inside the elastic of her panties, and he dragged them down her legs. She'd waxed her bikini line and trimmed her curls for a neat, sexy look. Now completely naked, completely vulnerable, she didn't move, hoping he liked what he saw.

He stared down at her. When he finally spoke, his voice sounded scratchy and raw. "You're staying the night, Ali. I'm going to fuck you until you can't walk."

Her whole body throbbed at his words. "I'm not going anywhere. Remember, I'm paying for the weekend."

His eyes darkened as he met her stare. "I don't want your money. I won't take it. I want you. *You*, I intend to take. Over and over again until you beg me to stop."

All she managed to do was gulp and nod in response. She couldn't imagine ever wanting him to stop.

"You prepared yourself for me, didn't you?" He petted her pussy, stroking her softly. "I like that. So sexy. So silky."

Her body ached for him, for his cock. She needed penetration.

"Spread your legs, Ali. Let me inside your cunt." He leaned over and his lips came down on hers again. His tongue entered her mouth, mirroring the movement that she'd craved for so long in more intimate places. Continuing to rub and pinch her nipples, she moaned, and her legs fell open.

Caleb took immediate advantage. His finger dipped into her, and her hips jerked at the jolt of pleasure that shook her body.

He raised his head. "Easy, sweetheart. Real easy. We're just getting started."

THREE

Caleb wanted nothing more than to fuck the hell out of Ali. He knew himself and knew he'd have a hard time holding back and not getting too rough with her. Although she seemed to get off on the idea of reckless, on-the-edge sex. "You're going to get fucked tonight, Ali, not made love to." He didn't intend to sugar-coat what she'd gotten herself into or what was about to happen to her.

"I know. That's what I want."

Damn. She was so incredibly hot, and she wanted it, was practically begging for it. He felt her limbs tremble. The look in her eyes showed determination but also wariness. Her trust in him struck hard. For the first time he could remember in ages, he felt unsure of what to do with a woman.

She curled her fingers around his upper arms. "Caleb, I want you to do it. I need you to do it."

Fuck. He felt the heavy beating of her heart. Its rhythm matched his own. "All right, Ali. But know that I'm not letting you out of this room until I'm through with you."

"O—okay."

After brushing her lips with a gentle kiss, he slid down her body and spread her legs. Starting softly, he placed wet kisses along her thighs. She squirmed beneath his mouth and let out little sounds of frustration and pleasure.

Moving closer to her pussy, his tongue swiped at the skin along the way. The scent of her arousal filled him. He wanted to devour this woman. He glanced up at her and saw that her eyes were squeezed shut. "Open your eyes, Ali. Watch me lick your cunt, baby."

Her eyes opened, and their gazes met. She looked incredibly sexy, needy, a little vulnerable. *And all mine.* He dipped his head between her legs and licked, his tongue intimately exploring her wet, delicious cunt.

A squeal of pleasure exploded out of her. She bucked her hips, her body demanding to be sated. "Oh, yes. Please! More!"

He gave it to her. With light swipes of his tongue, he tasted every inch of her pussy. Whenever he felt her getting close to climaxing, he'd pause and let her come back down.

"Caleb, keep licking me. I want to come!"

He knew making her wait, teasing her body mercilessly, would create a more powerful orgasm in the end. "You want to come, baby? Beg me for it." His tongue lightly circled her clit, causing her body to shake.

"Oh! Ah! Please, please, Caleb."

With her on the edge, he felt incredibly powerful. Sexually in control of her. He sucked and nibbled her clit, making her crazy, making her cry out in need. Now, he'd give her what she wanted.

"Caleb! Yes!" Her fingers gripped the sheets. She arched and gasped, squirming on the mattress. "Oh, oh, oh!" As he continued sucking her sensitive bud, her voice got higher and shriller. Her whole body spasmed, finally exploding in a massive climax.

Ah, yeah, baby. He'd definitely rocked her world. She would remember that orgasm for a long while. With a soft moan, she finally relaxed beneath him, and he raised his head.

While she lay recovering, he wiped his face then dug inside the nightstand drawer. She didn't even open her eyes at the sound of him moving around, just lay there breathing hard.

He needed to know how it felt to be gloved inside her cunt, and he couldn't wait any longer. He covered his shaft with a condom then positioned himself. Now that she'd been sated, she might have second thoughts about continuing. He didn't intend to give her the extra time to think about it. If that made him a bastard, then so be it. Without a word, he pushed his cock into her before she could change her mind about giving up her virginity. He plunged deep, breaking through her barrier.

Ali stiffened, and her eyes flew open.

He groaned. "Oh, fuck." Tight. Hot. Wet.

She grabbed his arms, and her nails dug into his skin.

The pain barely registered. Her pussy felt too good, her internal muscles gripping him like an iron fist. After he got himself under some control, he stared down into her wide eyes. "Are you okay?" He was careful not to move, to let her get used to the feel of him inside her. It almost killed him not to plunge repeatedly into her body, but he restrained himself, trying not to become the savage, yet, that called out to his baser instincts.

At his question, Ali nodded. That's about all she could do. So many feelings and emotions flooded through her. She felt completely . . . full . . . with Caleb inside her. He was so big!

And though his eyes looked caring, she recognized the banked fire behind the look.

The orgasm she'd experienced from his intimate licking had been like nothing she'd ever felt from her own hand. His entry had hurt more than she'd expected, but the pain was now slowly fading.

When she looked into his eyes, she felt a part of him. Okay, so that sounded like some silly storybook romance line, but she hadn't expected such intense emotion to accompany their physical joining.

"Ali?"

Carefully, she wrapped her legs around his hips to let him know that she still wanted him. He sank deeper inside her, and they both gasped. This time, her reaction came from pleasure, not pain. She raked her nails down his back and smiled when he shivered. This first time, with this man, she'd never forget.

"I'm okay, Caleb. You don't have to hold back." She wanted a great experience, but she really wanted him to have a great experience too. That's how she wanted him to remember her and this night, as a hot and sensual encounter.

He moved his hips forward and back, easily and slowly. His tongue traced the shell of her ear. "You're so tight, Ali. Being inside you, fucking you, feels incredible."

Oh, yes! Oh, goodness! The slight curve of his cock touched all her sensitive points when he pushed deep. She turned her head and kissed him. Their tongues touched and caressed. She tasted her own cum still lingering in his mouth. She actually enjoyed the flavor and swirled her tongue, trying to get more. Her legs tightened, and she pushed up against him.

He moaned and lowered his head to her neck, licking and kissing her heated flesh. He slowed his movements.

"Don't hold back," she repeated. "I need you. Fuck me!" The

plea she heard in her own voice surprised her. But she spoke the truth. She hungered for more. More of him. More of everything.

Caleb untangled her arms from around his shoulders. He pressed her hands down to the mattress on either side of her head and wrapped his fingers around her wrists. When he raised his head, his eyes burned into hers. "You want me to take you like some animal? Is that it?"

"Yes," she breathed out raggedly, her heart rate jumping. "I do. Fuck me, Caleb. Hard."

Caleb's blood rushed through his veins. She wanted it. He'd give it to her. His mouth swooped down on hers, and his tongue plundered her mouth, sweeping inside, tasting, commanding, taking what he craved. And giving back what she seemed to crave in return.

He pulled away, stared into Ali's desire-filled gaze and tightened his hold on her wrists. He pushed his cock deeply into her body, withdrew then plunged back in hard.

She gasped.

He groaned from the pure pleasure of fucking this woman. He withdrew halfway and stared into her eyes. When her lips parted to draw in a deep breath, he thrust into her again. Harder.

This time her gasp was louder, sharper.

Yeah. She did get off on being fucked hard, rough. With a growl of savage need, he pumped his hips, plunging into her like a man starved for a woman's body. For *her* body. Over and over, he thrust into her. Harder and harder. He couldn't get deep enough.

"Yes, Caleb!"

Her body spasmed around his. Her back arched, and cries of pleasure spilled from her lips. "Ohh!"

The sound of skin slapping against skin, along with her moans and heavy breathing, sent a wave of pure lust through him. When his eyes locked with hers, a deeper connection hit him than he'd ever expected. "Ali . . . " Her name tore from his lips.

Caleb released her wrists. He pinched her nipples, and she cried out again, louder, arched her back tighter. "That's right. Keep coming, baby."

"Yes!"

He pumped his hips faster, knowing she had more in her to give. Her cries of passion and the beautiful flush of sexual excitement on her body made him crave to give her as strong a climax as possible.

"I love it, Caleb! More!"

When she came a third time and screamed his name in her ecstasy, he lost it. "Oh, fuck!" A roar exploded from him as his body crested, and he toppled over the edge to join her in a climax so strong he nearly passed out.

They both lay gasping, trying to regain their breath. Finally, Caleb rolled off her. He took care of the condom then returned to the bed and dragged Ali against his side. "Are you okay?" His own limbs still felt shaky.

"Better than okay," she answered, her voice sounded winded.

"Sore?"

"Not that I can feel. All I feel right now is exhausted bliss." She glanced up at him with tears in her eyes.

He sucked in a sharp breath and didn't know what to say. He caressed her back and hip. "You'll feel it in the morning. Get some sleep." Emotions roiled inside him—caring, possession, need, protectiveness. Somehow, he felt the urge to say something more, something soft and soothing, to her. "Ali?"

When she didn't answer, he glanced into her face. Sound asleep.

Thinking about their night together, he pulled away from her and walked into the bathroom. After taking a leak and cleaning himself up, he grabbed a washcloth, ran lukewarm water over the cloth then squeezed it out. With a second, dry washcloth, he returned to the bedroom. What he couldn't put into words, he could express with at least a small amount of kindness.

Carefully, so as not to wake her, he cleaned her body. He hoped she wouldn't be too sore in the morning. The way she lay on the bed reminded him of an angel. The way she'd fucked him and begged for more was closer to pure sin.

He deposited the washcloths in the laundry basket then returned to stretch out beside her. He drew her closer and covered them both with the sheet and blanket.

No way was he letting this woman just walk out of his life. She might have only planned to lose her virginity tonight then go back to her everyday life without him, but he'd find some way to change her mind. He'd never come so hard with a woman, and he intended to have more than just one weekend of pleasure.

Caleb's eyes slowly opened, and he stretched languidly under the covers. He glanced toward the rays coming through the window. Normally, he hated mornings. Today, he looked forward to greeting the sun. A smile crossed his face. What a great night. He hadn't felt so content after a bout of sex in a long while. He turned onto his side, reaching for Ali at the same time.

The bed was empty.

He bolted upright. His gaze swept the room. Everything lay still and quiet. Her clothes were gone. He looked at the clock. Almost eight. Early. He plopped back down, and a wave of depression took hold.

Ali was gone. For how long, he wondered? He'd been so sated that he'd slept right through until morning.

"Well, okay, fine," he mumbled to himself, suddenly not so excited about the day after all. "It's over." She'd wanted her cherry popped. He'd done it. She'd left. Case closed. Except, damn it, he couldn't get her out of his mind and didn't want to just let her go.

He cringed, thinking how she might have allowed Ed Morton the same access to her body. She was one unique lady. She deserved the best of everything in her life. He was certainly far from the best, but somehow she made him want to be better. For her.

Fuck. He shook his head. Sex. That's all this was. Don't make the encounter into anything more, he told himself. Just because she embodied what he craved in a woman didn't mean their sleeping together might have grown into something more than physical if she'd stuck around. He admired her and enjoyed their time together. The sex had been fantastic. But he couldn't even really call her a friend. They didn't know each other well enough.

The smell of fresh coffee caught his attention. "What the hell?" He tossed back the covers. Was it possible?

After pulling on his robe, he followed the aroma to the kitchen. Ali sat at the table.

She hadn't left him. He felt like shouting "*Yes.*"

He stepped inside the arched entry. "Um, hi." Her clothes were different. She must have gone home, changed and then came back. He liked that she came back.

Her gaze snapped up to his. "Oh, hi." She scrambled up from the table. "Would you like some coffee?"

He slid into a seat. "Please. You left?"

She shrugged. "I went home, took a bath and changed clothes. I wasn't sure you'd want me here this morning. But then I felt strange about leaving without saying anything." She set a cup of coffee in front of him. "So I came back."

"Why would you think I wouldn't want you here? We could have showered together this morning. I'd love to slide my hands over your wet body and help you wash every inch of soft skin." He wiggled his eyebrows.

"Mmm, that does sound nice." A smile tugged at her lips. "I guess I just didn't want to intrude too much on your life."

"You're the one who wanted the weekend." When she frowned, he realized how that sounded. "And I want the weekend too. The whole weekend."

Her smile widened.

Beautiful. The fact that she'd returned and made herself comfortable in his kitchen gave him a warm feeling inside. Her presence made everything seem nicely domestic, like he lived in a real home instead of just a house. "Sit with me."

She sat across from him at the small oak table.

Suddenly wondering if another reason might exist for her leaving, concern rolled through him. "You are okay, right? I didn't hurt you last night, did I?" At one point, he'd been pretty rough with her.

"No, of course not." She reached for his hands. "You were great, Caleb. Making love with you was better than I ever imagined."

Making love—that's how she viewed it. He didn't know what to think. They'd fucked, pure and simple. But somehow . . . it did seem to be more than that.

"Thank you so much for everything."

He didn't know what to say. He cleared his throat, thinking he needed to say something profound, but came up empty. When he pulled his hands away, feeling inadequate, her smile faded and she actually looked hurt. An arrow of pain lodged in his heart.

Ali sat looking at her hands atop the table, not knowing what to say. Her body felt sated, but her emotions were one big jumble today. She'd love to explore a real relationship with Caleb, but she knew that kind of thing scared men off, so she wasn't about to say anything. They'd only spent one night together, after all. She didn't want to make him feel invaded or trapped or whatever a man felt when a woman pushed into his life too quickly.

Everything had gone great last night. She'd never forget the way he'd made her feel. She found it amazing, though, how the light of day could make things feel so unsettled.

She sighed and looked up at him, getting more confused by the moment. First, he'd tried to shoo her away, not wanting to sleep with her. Now, he seemed to want her around. Had their intimacy changed him? Or was that simply wishful thinking on her part? She didn't know. She only knew that making love with him had certainly changed her.

"Ali." He smiled gently. "This weekend is for fun, so let's have fun and not worry about anything else for now." He stood up and pulled her out of the chair. "Okay?"

He'd obviously picked up on her turbulent emotions. "Okay." When he hugged her tightly, she wrapped her arms around him. She'd enjoy all the time she could with Caleb and make some lifetime memories for herself this weekend. After that, she'd deal with whatever happened.

FOUR

As dusk settled outside, casting shadows around the room, Ali plopped down on Caleb's couch, feeling content. They'd spent a wonderful day together.

Caleb tossed his keys on the coffee table then flipped on a lamp. "Did you like the motorcycle ride?"

"I loved it." She'd felt completely free riding behind him. What a thrill! In fact, she'd felt so alive today with Caleb that returning to her old, mundane life as a librarian held little appeal.

"Thanks for taking me by the motorcycle shop. It was interesting to see where you work. The place looked bigger on the inside than it appeared from the street."

"I'm glad you liked it. We added on to the back end last year. One day I hope to solely own the shop and even expand to more cities in the area."

His eyes lit up as he spoke. She admired his passion for something he obviously loved.

"And now . . . " He tugged her to her feet. "My sexy beauty, enough about business." He cupped her cheek, stroking her skin with his thumb.

His words and touch took her breath away. Heck, just one look from him, with those "let's fuck" eyes, made her melt.

"The weekend isn't over yet. So what do you want to do? Lady's choice."

She chewed at her bottom lip a moment then released it. She knew exactly what she wanted, and she intended to let him know too before her time with him ended. "I want to learn how to properly . . . suck your dick."

His eyes widened, and a burst of husky laughter escaped him. "Oh, fuck, yeah." He grabbed her hand. "Come on."

Caleb brought out a more sensual side of her personality than she had ever realized existed, even in her fantasies. She followed him into the bedroom, eager to continue their erotic weekend.

A thought struck her. "Um, Caleb." She tugged a moment on his hand. "Wait. You don't think I'm just all sex crazed or something, do you?" she blurted. She wanted him to think of her as more than simply a warm body in his bed. Strange, actually, considering the dynamics of their relationship and what she'd originally approached him for, if you could even call what they had a relationship.

He sat down on the bed and laughed. And laughed. He held his stomach.

Somehow, she didn't find this all that funny. "Caleb!" She slapped at his shoulder. "Stop already." She didn't know if he was laughing at her, what she'd said or the whole situation.

"You, Ali, are a real jewel."

"What?" A jewel? That was a good thing, right?

He pulled her down beside him. "I haven't had such fun with someone in a long while."

"Truly?" Her whole body warmed.

"Truly."

She saw the honesty of his words in his eyes and in the smile on his face. She felt much the same about him. She'd needed excitement and fun in her life, and he had filled that need. She doubted she'd ever grow tired of a man like Caleb.

Feeling secure and confident, she reached for the button on his jeans. "Show me how to suck you off."

"You bet." He pulled his shirt over his head while Ali unzipped him. With her help, he shucked his jeans and briefs. He wrapped her hand around his semi-hard length. "Touch my dick, Ali. All over."

She knelt down on the carpet and lightly moved her fingers over him, examining the length, breadth and ridges of him with interest. She marveled at how much pleasure this one incredible organ had given her. Taking her time, she savored the feel of him. Velvet over steel. Pure male power.

Unable to wait any longer, she leaned over and kissed the tip of his cock. When he groaned, she lightly fingered his balls, wanting to increase his pleasure as much as possible.

"Ah, yeah. Nice and gentle. Lick my dick, Ali. I want to feel your tongue sliding down my shaft."

Her tongue darted out and stroked across the wide head of his purplish-red cock then eased down his long, thick shaft. She felt him stiffen and glanced up into his eyes.

"Again," he choked out.

She stroked him once more with the tip of her tongue, enjoying the musky taste of him. Unique.

"Lick my balls."

Slowly, she dragged her tongue down the length of his cock and back up again. Over and over. Then she glided her tongue over his balls with a light, gentle touch.

"Ah, fucking great, baby."

She'd never much liked when men called her baby. But with Caleb, the endearment made her feel special and warm inside. She experimented with different licks over his cock, paying special attention to his reactions. She found a spot on the underside of his cock just below the head that he seemed to like her licking the best, especially when she rapidly flicked her tongue.

"Oh, yeah, Ali. Wrap your fingers around the base now."

She curled her fingers around him. He reached down and covered her hand with his. Moving up and down his shaft, he showed her the stroking rhythm he liked.

Looking up at him, she watched him move, studied his body. Firm with just the perfect amount of muscle everywhere. His cock seemed incredibly thick. And he knew how to use it. He'd proven such a fabulous lover. She wished this weekend could go on forever.

"Enough stroking. Suck my dick now."

Yes. That sounded decadent and so sexually delightful that she smiled. Carefully, she wrapped her lips around the tip of his cock and sucked lightly. When he caressed her head and urged her to take more of him, she sucked another wonderful inch into her mouth. Addictive—Caleb was definitely addictive. Emotionally, she was sinking, becoming more and more attached to this man who showed her all about the physical side of love by tending just as carefully to her feelings.

"That's great, Ali. Just a little more suction. Ah, yeah. Perfect. Suck it. Yes."

Ali felt a huge sense of power and control over Caleb. While she enthusiastically sucked him, taking as much of his cock into her mouth as possible, she unbuttoned her blouse and slipped the garment off her shoulders. Her bra quickly followed. She felt sexier than she had ever imagined, kneeling semi-dressed, with her breasts bared, and eating Caleb's cock.

With a disappointed-sounding groan, he gently pushed her away and helped her to her feet. "Enough, or I'm going to come."

"I wouldn't have minded." She smiled sexily and ran her tongue across her lips.

"Damn," he groaned. "You're incredible, Ali. Next time, I'm coming down your throat. And you're going to swallow every fucking drop."

Ooo, that sounded good to her.

He reached for the zipper of her pants. "Get your clothes off."

The phone on the nightstand rang. Caleb frowned. He raised his finger, indicating for her to hang on, and scooted back to answer. Because of his business, he didn't want to take the chance of missing an important call. Though he was definitely tempted just to let the damn thing ring.

"Hello. Yeah, Rick. What's up?" His partner in the motorcycle shop usually called sometime during the weekend to let him know about any news. They'd missed Rick at the shop earlier, so he hadn't gotten the latest update. The man sounded cheerful, so all must be well.

Caleb pointed to Ali's pants. She raised an eyebrow, and he made a tugging motion with his hand. She smiled and continued undressing. *Oh, yeah. Show me some skin.*

"Huh? Oh, nothing much, Rick. Just watching a beautiful woman get naked."

She hesitated and that brow arched again. Caleb grinned and blew her a kiss.

With a soft laugh, she wagged her finger at him. But she must not have minded too much because she continued taking off her clothes.

He saw the erotic possibilities with Ali and wanted to explore as much as he could with her this weekend . . . longer, if she allowed it.

"Yeah, I'm listening. Go ahead."

Naked now, Ali crawled up on the bed.

Sexy, he mouthed to her, his dick hard and ready to plunge into her wet pussy.

"How do you want me?" she whispered into his ear, then sucked his lobe into her mouth. She made a sound very close to a purr.

Caleb shuddered at her words and actions. He liked her growing boldness. "Condom," he whispered.

She raised her head and nodded. Reaching over, she grabbed a foil square off the nightstand, opened the packet and, while he watched, rolled it over his cock.

He shouldered the phone and gripped her hips. Gently, he straddled her over his shaft and thrust deep. The muscles of her pussy gripped him tightly. He practically dropped the phone from the intensity of being gloved so snuggly inside her cunt. Rick said something about an order for five motorcycles, but the man's words didn't really register.

Ali moaned. She bit her lip, keeping the sound low. Caleb gritted his teeth. Ali was so hot, fucking him with Rick listening.

"Nail her good, bud," Rick said on the other end, with a low chuckle.

"Oh, yeah. I intend to."

"Intend to what?" she asked, rotating her hips.

"Ah . . . nice move. Rick and I want to nail you good, sweetheart." When her eyes dilated, and he saw her increased interest, his pulse raced. *She wants it.* He squeezed her breast.

"Mmm." She leaned close and licked at the tender skin right below his ear. "Okay . . . both of you."

At the erotic sensation, along with her words, he growled in response. While still holding the phone, he pinched one of her nipples until she moaned. "Ride me, Ali," he ordered in a no-nonsense tone, not bothering to hide his words, nor their actions, from Rick since she was obviously turned on by the idea of being with two men at the same time, even if one of them was on the other end of a phone line.

Without hesitation, she moved her hips, riding his cock with abandon, as if she'd done so a thousand times. Her fingers gripped his shoulders. "Oh, Caleb! Spank me!"

Caleb's whole body jerked at her sexy request.

"I heard that," Rick said over the phone. "Spank her, man. Hard. So I can hear it."

"It's going to sting," he told her.

"Do it, Caleb!"

He brought his palm down hard on one of her ass cheeks. Too hard? The crack sounded loud, even to his own ears.

Ali and Rick both groaned.

Since she didn't protest the swat, he continued spanking her hard and now also fast. Each slap brought him closer to losing it. "Damn, you are so sexy, Ali. And you're getting off on another man listening to us fuck, aren't you? What else turns you on?" The possibilities made his mouth water and his dick feel as hard as steel.

"I'll try anything you want, Caleb."

"Anything?" He fought for control.

She nodded. "I want it all."

"You've got a live one there, bud. Let me talk to her while you fuck her," Rick said. "We'll see what she's got in her."

Intrigued, Caleb handed Ali the phone. "Listen to him."

Ali cocked an eyebrow then took the phone and put it to her ear. She was close to coming, and her ass tingled from the spanks Caleb gave her. The idea of doing something kinky with him appealed to her newly found sense of adventure.

Caleb's fingers curled around her hips and he plunged his cock repeatedly into her pussy.

"Oh, yes!" She loved the feel of his cock thrusting deep inside her, touching all her sensitive areas.

Rick chuckled in her ear. "You like it nasty. I can tell."

"Yes," she moaned, without thinking about her response. All she could think about was the pleasure rolling through her body.

"Say, 'I want it nasty, Caleb,' right now," Rick ordered her. "Go on, say it."

"I want it nasty, Caleb," she repeated, unable to stop herself. She needed this sexual intensity and the feeling of recklessness in her life, at least once.

"Oh, yeah. How nasty, baby?" Caleb asked her.

"Say, 'Fuck my ass' . . . tell him."

"Ah!"

"Say it!"

"Fuck my ass." Her voice sounded shaky, but she wanted Caleb to do it. The image in her head of his cock pushing up her asshole, her totally submitting to the act, brought her close to coming. "Fuck my ass, Caleb!"

Rick groaned into the phone. "Man, I'd love to see him pumping his cock into a luscious asshole."

Caleb immediately stopped thrusting into her pussy. His eyes grew more intense than she'd ever seen before. He lifted her off his cock and pushed her face down onto the mattress. "You're going to get the ass-fucking of a lifetime, baby."

"Yes, yes, yes . . . " she practically wailed. Anticipation filled her. Would she even be able to take his thick cock up her ass?

His hand smacked her ass cheeks, one then the other, over and over, until she squirmed and whimpered.

"Oh, Caleb!"

He lubricated her asshole with her own cream. He pushed one and then two fingers into the tight opening to prepare her for his cock.

Her hips bucked. "Oh, damn, that feels good."

"Is he doing it?" Rick asked.

"Yes," she whimpered, loud enough for Rick to hear. "With his fingers." The feeling of Caleb's fingers stretching her hole, pumping in and out, deep then shallow, hard then soft, was a feeling she'd never even imagined before.

She heard Rick's heavy breathing over the phone . . . along with another sound. Yes. He was masturbating. Sexy!

"Tell him to shove his fat cock up your hole now," he ordered.

His harsh words caused her already pounding heart to race out of control. She glanced over her shoulder, as turned on as he was, and as she hoped Caleb was too. "Use your cock. Fuck my hole, Caleb. Now!"

"Damn, Ali!" Sweat had formed on his chest and brow, and his hands shook slightly. He spread her ass wide and pressed the head of his cock against her puckered hole. Slowly, he pressed forward until the head popped inside.

"Oh! Yes! Push your cock deeper. All the way up my ass. Do it."

Rick groaned. "I'm going to come."

Caleb pushed deeper then pumped her ass in short, fast strokes. His fingers played with her clit. "Come for us, Ali. Come."

"Come, sexy baby," Rick groaned.

Her body spasmed, and her asshole gripped Caleb's dick hard, ripping a moan from his lips. When her pussy contracted, she screamed. A powerful orgasm shot through her.

Rick and Caleb shouted as they came at almost the same time. Their groans filled her ears, and she came again, once more milking Caleb's dick with her ass.

His body shook, and his fingers dug into her hips, holding her tightly. "Fuck, yeah!"

After what seemed like forever, she collapsed on the mattress, totally spent. Rick was quiet on the other end of the phone. Caleb lay silently across her back, until finally he shifted to the side with a grunt and hung up the phone.

His hand lightly stroked her ass, but that's as far as he moved. Feeling exhausted and unable to move, she barely managed to mumble a few words of thanks for the incredible experience. Too tired to even clean up, her eyelids gradually lowered, and she drifted off to sleep.

Ali jerked awake, not sure what had roused her. The morning light streamed through the window. The weekend was over.

Disappointment rolled over her like a suffocating wave. She'd so enjoyed her time with Caleb. She never wanted it to end. He'd shown her an incredible world of sex and given her a greater sense of self.

When she made a move to get up, a sharp slap to her butt made her squeal. She glanced behind her. "Caleb, what are you doing?"

"Getting your attention. It took three swats to wake you. Up on your knees, Ali. I'm horny as hell from looking at you lying there naked and thinking about last night. You're getting an early morning fuck, baby."

Oh, my! He was positioned in back of her, ready to go. When she faced front, she saw his intense expression reflected in the mirrored headboard as he stared down at her body. His cock stood hard and already gloved in a condom. None too gently, he pulled her to her knees.

Her heart hammered against her ribs. One last fuck before he tossed her out? If so, she was determined to enjoy it.

With a hard plunge, he pushed his cock as deeply as he could get it into her pussy. "Oh, yeah. You're so incredibly tight. I've been thinking of getting inside your beautiful cunt since I woke up."

His words sent a delicious thrill right through her. Ali hung her head and moaned. This position made his penetration feel so powerful.

He pulled halfway out and pushed back in hard.

She thought she heard him growl, like the wild predator she'd always imagined him to be. She moaned his name, loving the way he took sexual charge.

He plunged into her hard once more, pushing deep. "You like that?" He ground his hips against her.

"Yes, Caleb." This was the bad boy in full form. Pure sex, without holding back.

"I want to hear you beg for it." He tangled the fingers of one of his hands in her hair. "Say, *fuck me hard.* Say it, Ali." He didn't ask, he ordered, tightening his hold on her.

His eyes burned into hers, connecting in the mirror. She gulped. "Fuck me. Fuck me hard, Caleb." Words turned him on, and she wanted to turn Caleb on, big time.

He pulled halfway out and slapped her ass. "Louder." He thrust back into her.

"Oh!"

His fingers released her hair and curled around her hips. He began plunging repeatedly into her pussy. "Say it, Ali!"

Her body shook, and she felt right on the edge of coming. "Yes! Fuck me hard! Hard! Oh, yeah. Like that. Ooo, rougher. Ah, oh! Faster, Caleb! Make me come!" The words spilled from her mouth.

"Yeah!" He pumped her like some sexual savage. "You love it like this, don't you, Ali? Hard, fast, nasty."

"I—"

He spanked her ass. "You're so good, baby. Damn, I love your tight cunt."

Ali's heart felt ready to explode. She gulped in lungfuls of air. "Yes, more!"

"Yeah . . . I'll give you more." He thrust into her with powerful strokes, showing no mercy.

"Yes! Caleb!" She couldn't get enough of him. A flutter of pleasure started inside her pussy and raced through her body with an intensity and speed she'd never felt before. "Ahhhh!"

"Yeah. Come for me, Ali! Come hard."

"Ohhh!" Her world exploded, her orgasm so intense she screamed his name and felt on the verge of falling into a never-ending vortex of sexual ecstasy.

In response, Caleb roared. His body tensed, and his fingers gripped her hips almost painfully. "Yes, Ali! Yes!" He came long and hard. "Ah! Fucking incredible!"

They both collapsed on the bed, breathing heavily. Ali couldn't move, completely conquered, sexually.

After a few moments, Caleb kissed her temple.

She lay quietly for quite a while then looked over at him. "Um, can we do it again, Caleb?"

A groan rumbled up from his throat. "Again? You're going to kill me, Ali, I swear."

She grinned. She trusted Caleb completely, with her body and with her emotions. She'd never realized the power and thrill of sex and wanted to experience it over and over again, as much as possible. But whenever she looked at Caleb, she also wanted so much more than just sex. Did he?

She supposed she'd find out soon, for as soon as she left his bed, the weekend would officially be over.

EPILOGUE

Six Months Later

Ali looked around the large, grassy field in the middle of nowhere. "Why did we come all the way up here?" she asked Caleb, who stood securing their helmets on the motorcycle.

They'd continued to see each other after that first weekend. She wasn't exactly sure how it had all happened, or who had made the first move. Being together just seemed so natural. She looked forward to their time together each and every day. And he'd shown her a remarkable world of sexual pleasures she'd never dared to imagine.

Sometimes they stayed at his place, sometimes her place. And she'd become really close with two of his sisters, who had turned out to be avid readers, just like her. The last six months had been some of the best in her life.

Things had been a little awkward at his motorcycle shop with Rick the first time she'd stopped by for a visit after the phone sex incident. But they'd worked it out, especially after she'd found out the man was gay. She hadn't felt uncomfortable around him after that. Secretly, she thought he had a crush on Caleb, but she never mentioned her feelings.

"Isn't it beautiful up here? Peaceful?"

"Yes." She took in a big breath of clean air. The massive oak trees, probably hundreds of years old, caught her attention.

"I bought it."

"What? This field?" He'd never mentioned an interest in owning land.

"Yep. I've decided to build a house up here. I'm tired of the city. It's too hectic."

Her heart and emotions plummeted. Talk about the rug being pulled out from under a person. "Oh." He was moving away. Not to a different city, but still far enough away where they wouldn't see each other daily like now. Maybe she'd crowded him without realizing it, so he'd decided to put some space between them. "This location is quite a distance from town."

"I know, but I fell in love with the area when I saw it. I couldn't resist." He touched her arm. "Hey, what's wrong? You don't like it?"

She tried to force a smile. "It's beautiful here, Caleb. It's just that—" She'd fallen in love with him, totally and completely, and didn't want to let him go. She shrugged and held back a sniffle. She refused to cry in front of him. If this was his dream, she wasn't going to spoil his excitement. "Will you be happy living out here all alone?"

"No. But . . . I'll be happy if you live out here with me."

"What?" Her voice caught. She swallowed hard. "You want me to move out here with you?"

"More than that." He knelt in front of her and took her hand. "I want you to marry me, Ali. I love you."

Love. Her heart raced, and she could hardly think straight. Tears misted her eyes. "Oh, Caleb. Are you certain?"

"Certain that I love you? Yes. Certain that I want you to be my wife and share my life with me? Yes. Now, please don't torture me. Please say yes to me, Ali."

"Yes! Yes, I'll be your wife." Joy exploded inside her. "I love you so much, Caleb."

Caleb rose and swung her into his arms. "Yes!"

They both erupted into laughter.

Ali had known that approaching Caleb with her plan would change her life. But falling in love with him had made her happier than she'd ever believed possible. And now, as Caleb's soon-to-be wife, she knew that in life fantasies really did come true.

He walked them out into the field. "Let me show you where the master bedroom is going to be . . . "